THE
DISCOVERY

THE
DISCOVERY

GORDON HILL

Published 2017
by Gordon Hill

ISBN 978-0-473-41868-7

Printed by The Copy Press, Nelson, New Zealand. www.copypress.co.nz

To my loving wife, Patti Marie Hill,
for all her love and support.

To lecturer, Richard Brookes,
for all his encouragement.

chapter one

IMAGES OF THE ALIENS

December 14th 1972

American astronaut Gene Cernan prepares to ignite the assent engine of the lunar module, codenamed Challenger. He and fellow astronaut and geologist Harrison Schmitt, had travelled thirty five miles in their lunar rover, and collected a total of one hundred and ten kilograms of moon rock from a region on the moon known as Taurus Littrow. It was another attempt to learn more about the origin of earth's heavenly companion and man's quest to find the possibility of life on another world, or if he is destined to wonder through the universe alone forever. Now, both men were about to bring down the curtain on the Apollo Moon programme, as Apollo 17 was planned to be the final Moon landing. It had been a series of missions that had both brought tragedy as well as triumph. The deaths of astronauts Gus Grissom, Roger Chaffee, and Edward White in the Apollo 1 fire five years earlier, had brought an even more determined approach from N.A.S.A to reach John Kennedy's goal of placing a man on the moon by the end of the nineteen sixties.

Back on earth, the technical team at mission control scrutinized the instrument panels on their computers. They were waiting anxiously for the radio signals from the command module code named America, and its pilot, Ron Evans. Neither Cernan nor the mission controllers could give the go-ahead to launch the lunar module until the command ship had emerged from the far side of the moon.

On board the command module, Evans gazed out the window of his spacecraft at the crater scarred surface of the moon sixty miles below him. He wondered when men would return to this desolate world which humans had looked upon since the dawn of man. Would they return in Evans's life time and for what purpose? Would it be America, or another country that would make the journey? This was something he had no answer for. That was for the future, but the time was now, and Evans had to concentrate on matters at hand. Checking the telemetry of his craft, he gazed out the window once more, then the most welcoming site for any Apollo astronaut came into view in the centre window of the spacecraft. The planet Earth rising majestically over the moons horizon, the beautiful blue of its oceans and the white swirling clouds could clearly be seen even at that distance. Evans had travelled alone around the dark side of the moon completely cut off from the world and his two companions, but now, although a quarter of a million miles away, the site of the good Earth made the American feel close to home and the people he loved. He flicked the switch on his microphone and with a loud voice called out to mission control.

"Houston, this is America, do you read over? Houston this is America do you read?"

The mission control was a hive of activity. Over a hundred people manned the centre, but it was Major Charles Fullerton the capsule communicator or cap-com for short who was waiting for Evans to call in.

"This is cap-com reading you loud and clear Ron, good to have you back," said Fullerton.

"Roger Houston," replied Evans.

While Evans and the command ship raced towards Taurus Littrow, Cernan and Schmitt waited patiently in the cramped lunar module, their eyes fixed on the instrument panel of the spacecraft. Hearing Evans's voice over the radio, Cernan called out.

"Reading you loud and clear America. This is Challenger we're coming up on two minutes ten seconds for lift off."

Cernan then turned to Schmitt and in a calm voice said. "Jack check your power breaker."

"Okay," replied Schmitt. Once again the co-pilot checked all circuit breakers that supplied the power for lift off were armed. "We're good Gene," he said confidently.

Cernan then pulls a small lever to the left of the main control panel and instantly two lights flicker above him on the overhead control board.

"Okay the master engine arm is on, I've got two good lights."

As the two men waited for Evans to arrive at the correct position for the two spacecraft's to rendezvous, the tiny camera mounted on the lunar rover overlooked the entire area. The spidery looking lunar module sat motionless on the lunar surface, its outer skin made from the thinnest of aluminium foil, glistened in the sun light. Mountains that had for millions of years been bombarded by tiny particles of meteoric dust to give them their soft rounded shape appear in the distance. In the words of Buzz Aldrin, Magnificent desolation.

"Okay Houston," called out Cernan. "Sequence ninety nine processed, three, two, one ignition."

The assent engine exploded into life, sending hundreds of pieces of the descent stage flying in all directions as the tiny craft pulled clear of its landing section.

"We're on our way, Houston," shouted Schmitt, as he and Cernan were carried into orbit to rendezvous with Evans. As the tiny fiery light from the assent engine began to diminish into the black void of space, once again all was still on the moon. To the world, Apollo 17 was the final Moon mission, yet unknown to us all there was a stealthy undertaking being planned, in a secret place, by secret people.

October 24th, 1962

The Cold War between the two superpowers, the United States of America and the Soviet Union, has reached a terrifying situation. On October 10th an American U.2 reconnaissance aircraft spotted Russian cargo ships on course for Cuba. They are believed to be carrying Russian SS-4 nuclear missiles, and if installed on these islands the communists would have missile launch sites just ninety miles from the coast of Florida. President John F. Kennedy has set the United States military to Defcon 3, while Cuban leader Fidel Castro modularizes his forces. Kennedy has quarantined Cuba by ordering a naval blockade of the island, and has demanded that Russian Premier Nikita Khrushchev remove the missiles. While the world is teetering on the brink of war, C.I.A agent Steve Curtis hides in the desolate landscape of Kazakhstan, south Russia. One mile east of Curtis's position lies the Baikanour Cosmodrome rocket base, home of the Russian space program. Curtis has been sent to observe the launch of the latest Russian space probe. It is believed that the Russians have developed a more powerful rocket which will enable them to launch heavier payloads. If this information is accurate, Russia could launch larger nuclear warheads as well as more sophisticated spy satellites. This is a disturbing time for the United States, as the Soviet Union is already leading the space race. Eighteen months ago they placed the first man into orbit around the earth, now rumour has it that a two-man spacecraft is being designed by their chief engineer. The Americans however are determined to close the gap. President Kennedy has laid down the challenge to the American people to place a man on the moon before the end of the decade. He feels it is important the supremacy of space be held by the flag of freedom for the safety of the world.

Curtis looks at his watch. He can just make out its face in the darkness of the cold Russian night.

"Eleven o'clock," he says to himself. "Where the hell is he?"

Curtis is waiting to make contact with Sergei Tarelkin, a Russian who has worked with Curtis many times since he and a group of Russian prisoners were rescued by the American agent three years earlier. Tarelkin has hated the communist way of life since his father, Professor Aleksandra Tarelkin, was taken away from him and his mother by the K.G.B when Sergei was only ten years old. Aleksandra's crime was to write an article objecting to the cost of Russian military might, when there was so much poverty across the Soviet Union. Curtis had been on the ground for the last twelve hours after parachuting from an army transport plane. He had walked eight miles to his present position across the desolate landscape of Kazakhstan to arrive at the rocket base by midday. Curtis was used to harsh terrain. The Amazon jungle, the Middle East and many more desolate areas of the world were familiar places to this experienced agent. It was no problem for the thirty-five year old, six-foot-one American to walk for miles. A ten mile jog every morning in his home town of Denver, Colorado, was something he had done since he was a schoolboy before joining the United States Air Force at the age of twenty one. Now a member of the C.I.A, Curtis is one of America's top agents.

During the afternoon, Curtis had surveyed the rocket base with high powered binoculars. To the west of the complex stood rocket silos surrounded by an array of different sized buildings.

Some of them looked old and abandoned but new larger structures, probably housing the latest Russian missiles, looked as if they'd been recently constructed.

To the east stood new launch pads with their giant gantries soaring over a hundred feet high, waiting for the next space rocket to be sent into orbit. A large assembly building stood two miles away from these launch areas, with a railway track connecting them. To stop the exhaust of the rocket rebounding from the ground and destroying the space vehicle, a flame trench was constructed beneath every gantry to deflect the rocket's tail fire. The American had watched the large doors of the assembly building slide open. Mounted horizontally on the back of a large railway vehicle the Russian R7 space rocket emerged into the sunlight. It was a complex machine comprising of a central core containing four main engines and four small guidance rockets. Clustered around the central core were four tapered booster engines which would be jettisoned minutes after take-off. A latticework arrangement attached the engine section to the upper stage which carried the payload, which could either be a satellite, space capsule, or even a nuclear warhead.

Curtis decided to rest for a while. Replacing his binoculars into his rucksack, he sat behind a large rock which was casting a shadow big enough for him to shelter from the heat of the sun.

Taking a flask of water from the side pouch, he took a drink to wash the desert dust from his throat. As he rested he began to wipe away the sweat from his forehead and his thick black hair line. He gazed across the barren landscape, and began to think of the events taking place off the coast of Cuba. He thought about the terrible consequences of a nuclear war, which neither country would win. His mind recalled his days as a fighter pilot in Korea, shooting down enemy aircraft and killing pilots whose faces he never saw. He thought hard about the commitment he had shown to his country and the terrible loss of his friends. All in the name of freedom. Now, once again, the world was on the brink of war. It seemed the more mankind advanced technologically, the more dangerous he became. Curtis had no time to think about man's stupidity; after all he had given many years of his life to military action and espionage. It seemed hypocritical for him to complain when he was so much a part of it all, he thought to himself. Putting his thoughts aside, he decided to check out the base once more. Taking his binoculars from his rucksack and emerging from behind the rock, he looked towards the rocket base. The heat of the sun had created a shimmering haze across the landscape. This, together with the dust created by the constant motion of military vehicles, made the visibility quite poor. Nevertheless he could make out that the R7 was now standing in a vertical position. A powerful hydraulic piston on the transport vehicle had raised the space rocket over the flame trench. Four umbilical arms with work platforms attached to them, had swung into position around the spacecraft, holding the vehicle stable. Now technicians were busily working on fuelling the rocket and Curtis realized that it was only a matter of time before another Russian space vehicle would head into orbit. As the hours had passed, Curtis felt the temperature of the day change rapidly. Night-time had brought a biting cold wind and the American searched through his rucksack for a thick camouflage jacket.

"That's better," he thought to himself as he zipped up the replica Russian army jacket. The garment gave some protection from the cold, but if Tarelkin didn't show soon, Curtis would be in for a long uncomfortable night.

Then a noise from the west gained the American's attention. Headlights from a Russian army vehicle were heading in his direction. Quickly grabbing the rucksack, he made his way to the large rock that had sheltered him from the sun earlier that day. The vehicle stopped about fifty yards from where he was hiding. A tall slim man dressed in a Russian army uniform climbed out. He stood by the door of the truck for a few moments, looking around him in all directions, checking if he'd been followed.

He began to walk around the area, carefully peering behind each rock. It was obvious to Curtis that the soldier knew that the C.I.A agent was in the vicinity. Slowly the American unzipped his thick camouflage jacket and reached inside. Withdrawing a Smith and Wesson from his shoulder holster, Curtis slowly moved from behind the large rock. He moved towards the soldier who was looking out in the direction of the rocket base. With both hands firmly gripping the butt of the gun he raised the weapon, bringing the gun's sites in line with the back of the soldier's head. Suddenly the Russian began to speak in a calm deep voice.

"Curtis, if you intend to take a man by surprise you must learn to do it much quieter than that."

"Sergei?" said a surprised Curtis.

"I didn't think it would be like you to shoot a man in the back," said the Russian turning around. Curtis lowered his gun and walked toward his old friend. The men shook hands. It had been some time since the two of them had worked together.

"It's good to see you again Steve, you're looking well," said the twenty eight year old Russian.

"Yes, it's good to see you too. How did you know it was me?"

"We received a coded message from Washington this morning giving your grid reference. I had a good idea you wouldn't be far from the base."

"Okay Sergei, your message was received by the C.I.A two days ago telling them you wanted to see me here."

"That's right."

"Okay, so what's it about? Is it something to do with those Russian ships heading towards Cuba?"

"No, it's something bigger than that," said the Russian.

Curtis couldn't believe what the Russian was saying. "Sergei, President Kennedy is prepared to blow those Russian ships out of the water and possibly start world war three. Are you telling me there's something bigger than that?"

"I think so, and so do my people. Your President has set America the challenge of reaching the moon before this decade ends has he not?"

"Yes."

"What I have to show you Curtis, is so important that it means your country must reach the moon before the Soviet Union."

The American agent was confused but obviously interested.

"Well, what the hell is it?"

At that moment a terrific roar came from the cosmodrome and both men turned towards the rocket base. The R7 space rocket's engines had ignited. As the roar became louder the four umbilical arms holding the rocket in position folded backwards simultaneously.

Immediately the rocket lifted off from its launch pad, and the whole area was lit up by the rocket's tail fire. As it gained altitude, it wasn't long before the vehicle was a tiny ball of fire accelerating across the blackness of the night sky.

"That's the reason, Steve. That's the reason you're here."

"Sergei I'm completely baffled about all this," said Curtis who was now more confused than ever.

Tarelkin looked at his watch.

"Look, I'll explain everything when we're underway. I have to get you out of here and to your rendezvous point. You're being picked up in fifty minutes time."

As Tarelkin made his way to the truck, Curtis ran to the rock to collect his rucksack. He ran to the passenger side of the cab and climbed in.

Tarelkin started the engine and soon had the vehicle heading down the dusty track away from the rocket base. Looking out through the side window Curtis gazed up at the night sky. It was a perfectly clear night and thousands of stars shone brilliantly like tiny particles of silver scattered across black velvet. There was a full moon that night, and it shone so brilliantly that the entire landscape could be seen for miles. As the truck rocked from side to side as it struck small stones and potholes, Curtis looked across at Tarelkin.

"Sergei, what's going on?"

Tarelkin, concentrating hard on the road in front of him, began to tell Curtis the reason why he needed to see him.

"For the last three months my country has been sending probes to photograph the moon. At first we thought our scientists were planning to land a craft on the surface."

"Okay," said Curtis listening carefully.

"Well, four months ago a probe was photographing an area of the moon known as Sinus Medii. All was going well until the controllers at Baikanour tried to alter the angle of the spacecraft with one of its thruster rockets."

Curtis now became interested. "What happened?"

"The thruster rocket jammed, sending the probe on a collision course for the moon. Thinking all was lost the scientists and technicians came to terms with the fact that they were going to lose their spacecraft, but they overlooked one thing."

"And that was?"

"On its descent the cameras were still taking pictures and transmitting them back to earth. It was when they processed the photographs they couldn't believe what they saw."

"Okay what was it?" said Curtis

Tarelkin pointed to a large envelope which was resting in the glove compartment beneath the dashboard. "Take a look at those," he said.

Curtis took the envelope and opened it. He withdrew four eight by ten inch black-and-white photographs. The images were rather poor quality but the American agent could make out that the prints were photographs of a desolate landscape.

"What am I supposed to be looking at?"

"You're looking at the crater known as Ukert in the Sinus Medii region of the moon. Inside this crater you can just see a small shiny object. Now, this is photograph 8B."

Curtis scanned his eyes across the print. He saw the tiny dot, but he still remained baffled as to what this was all about. "Okay, I can see it."

"Now, take a look at the second photograph, 8C. This was taken approximately one minute after the first. The thruster rocket had now jammed, and the vehicle was on a collision course with the moon. Notice the object getting larger in the frame."

Curtis looked at the second print. "Okay, I see it," repeated Curtis.

"Now look at the third photograph, 8D. You can now make out surface detail in the object, can you not?"

Curtis looked carefully at the third print. Although he was still unsure of what it was, he became more interested in the shiny object which was standing on the lunar surface.

He sat up and turned to Tarelkin. "Yes, there's something there alright. Have any of the Russian scientists got any idea what it could be?"

"Well you take a look at the last print, 8E."

Looking at the final print, Curtis was amazed to see a perfectly round object, shining as it reflected the sun light.

"What the hell?" said Curtis in disbelief. "I don't believe it."

"What do YOU think it could be?" said the Russian. The people at the rocket base believe it could be a crashed spacecraft but they are not sure.

Curtis looked at the surface detail and he could make out geometry in the object. "This thing must be huge." He said quietly.

"Not a natural phenomenon Curtis. Its alien, and the Russians want it," said Tarelkin. Think of it Curtis, it's advanced and in the hands of the Russians they would have something over you if they got to it first would they not?"

"I've got to get back to Langley with this. Sergei, is this missile business in Cuba a front for all this?"

Tarelkin shook his head. "No, Khrushchev knows nothing about this. A special group of scientists have been assembled to find out what the object is, but for sure the Cuban missile crisis keeps the minds of the Americans on something else while we explore that object."

"So who's the top man?"

"According to my contact at the base, one man has been put in charge. He's probably KGB but we have yet to find out exactly who he is."

"You say you have a contact at the base?"

"Yes, he is a chemical engineer working on their new rocket fuel. It creates more thrust than conventional fuel, but the only problem is it is highly toxic. Many of the technicians fuelling the rockets have died inhaling its deadly fumes."

"Right, I'll report back to our people at the C.I.A and see what they make of all this."

Tarelkin continued to drive along the dusty track towards Curtis's rendezvous point. The American agent placed the photographic prints back into the envelope, and leant forward to pick up his rucksack. Suddenly a tremendous flash and deafening explosion emitted only yards from the truck. A small artillery shell had missed the cab by inches and struck the road side sending dirt and fragments of missile in all directions. Shrapnel smashed into the windscreen as the truck spun out of control. Spinning sideways off the dirt track the vehicle turned over and burst into flames. The cab quickly began to fill with smoke and both men had to work fast or suffocate.

"Quick Sergei, the windscreen, kick it out," shouted Curtis.

With their backs pressed hard against their seats, the two men raised their knees to their chests.

"Okay, both together," shouted Curtis.

Thrusting their feet into the already damaged windscreen, Curtis and Tarelkin began to kick out the window panel.

The smoke was getting thicker and the heat more intense as both men kicked out the remaining glass. Curtis picked up his rucksack containing the photographs and threw it towards the roadside before climbing through the gap. Tarelkin followed, gasping for breath as he threw himself clear of the burning truck. Immediately machinegun fire opened up to the right of their position.

"Come on, Sergei," shouted Curtis as he grabbed the Russian by the collar and pushed him towards a ditch at the side of the road. As both men pushed their bodies hard against the ground, Curtis looked across at Tarelkin. "Are you alright?"

"Yes I'll be okay," he replied, as he began to take deep breaths of clean air.

"Stay down, I'll be back," said Curtis as he quickly thrust himself out of the ditch. As the bullets slammed into the dusty bank behind them, Curtis, keeping the burning vehicle between himself and the barrage of bullets, ran towards the trailer section of the truck. Carefully peering from behind it, he could see tiny flashes of gunfire from a small hill about two hundred yards away. He turned and ran back to the ditch.

"There's too many of them for us to handle. Any idea who they are?"

"They're probably a small unit from the rocket base. If they arrest us and find we are in possession of these photographs, we're finished."

Suddenly with a roar and whoosh of tail fire, a small artillery rocket shot across the top of the two men and towards the enemy position. There was a flash followed by a deafening explosion. The screams of soldiers could be heard as fire engulfed them. Curtis looked up and saw two of the men running away from the area, their bodies completely ablaze with fire. Another rocket quickly followed the first, crashing into the enemy position. Flames and thick smoke poured from the area permanently silencing the gunfire as quickly as it had begun. As the noise and dust began to settle, Curtis looked behind him. Carefully climbing from the ditch he saw a young Russian dressed in the similar uniform to Tarelkin running towards him. Immediately Curtis raised his gun and aimed straight at the soldier.

"Wait," shouted Tarelkin, as he leaped from the ditch and grabbing Curtis's arm. "Mikhail?"

Called Tarelkin as he began to run towards the young Russian, while another four rebels came out of hiding to join them. Curtis sighed with relief as it became clear that the young man was a friend of Tarelkin's. He placed his gun back into its shoulder holster and quickly walked towards the group.

"That was bloody close," he said. "It's obvious they know we're here, so we'd better get moving."

"Steve, this is Mikhail Dezhurov, and these are the rest of my men," said Tarelkin.

"I'm glad you made it in time," said Curtis as he shook Dezhurov's hand.

"I'm pleased to meet you comrade. Have you been injured?"

"No I'm fine thanks. Look Sergei, I think we better get out of here, there's no telling how many Russian soldiers there are in this area."

"We have horses nearby, are you all right with that Curtis?" asked Dezhurov.

"No problem, I've ridden horses since the age of ten. Just lead the way."

The seven men scrambled across the rocks to the six horses whose reigns had been tied to a large rock.

"You will share my horse, Mr Curtis," said the smallest of the rebels. "He's very strong, he'll be able to carry the two of us."

Curtis, Tarelkin and the five rebels mounted the horses and began to ride west.

High above Kazakhstan a transport plane had been sent from an American air base in Turkey. Captain Michael Hale and flight Lieutenant Dennis Gray kept radio silence throughout their flight.

"Fifteen minutes to contact," said Gray as his eyes scanned the instrument panel.

Down on the ground, Curtis, who had lots of experience riding horses, was finding the task much harder across the Kazakhstan landscape in the dark, with one of the rebels sharing the horse with him.

Dezhurov raised his right arm gesturing to the others to stop and hold their position. Each rider brought his horse to a halt and waited for a moment.

"What's wrong?" asked Curtis.

Tarelkin dismounted and walked towards him. "We wait here and listen."

Curtis dismounted his horse and waited a moment. Tarelkin pointed out towards the open plain. "This is your rendezvous point. Out there is a clearing large enough to land your aircraft. You'll have to move quickly when the plane lands. It is important that you are not on the ground too long. The radars at the rocket base can hear a pin drop, so you'll have to be out of here as quickly as possible."

"Got it," replied Curtis. "What about you and your men?"

"Don't worry about us. We know this land better than most and we know where to hide."

Curtis and the rebel group waited anxiously for the aircraft to arrive. Suddenly, west of their position, came the sound of a four engine turboprop transport plane.

"It's them," said Curtis.

Dezhurov and the other four rebels rode out onto the flat wasteland. They then separated till they were approximately a hundred yards from each other. Bringing his horse to a halt,

Dezhurov withdrew a flare pistol from the inside pocket of his jacket. Aiming the pistol into the air he fired a red flare skywards.

The other rebels immediately followed by releasing their flares, illuminating the entire area for the aircraft to make its landing.

On the flight deck the two American pilots looked out of the cockpit windows searching for the landing beacon. Flight Lieutenant Gray peered out of the starboard side of the aircraft.

"There, two o'clock," he shouted.

Captain Hale looked to the area where his co-pilot was pointing. "That's it, take her down. I don't want to be on the ground too long. They could shoot us down as we try to take off if we allow them to get in range."

Pulling back on the throttle controls and applying the air brakes, the two pilots carefully guided the aircraft into the area.

"Lower the undercarriage," said Hale.

Gray lent forward and slid the undercarriage control lever down. Curtis and the rebels watched as the giant transport plane began to slowly descend.

"Undercarriage down and locked," said Gray.

As Hale banked the aircraft to the right for the final approach, Gray placed his hands around the throttle controls and began to reduce the speed. Slowly the aircraft descended, and the rough rugged terrain crept nearer.

"Let's hope we don't hit any sharp stones. If we rip the tyres to pieces we'll never get off the ground," said Gray.

"That's the chance we have to take I'm afraid, replied Hale. "Here we go."

The four large turboprops caused clouds of dust to spiral over the aircraft, as the rear undercarriage made contact with the dry ground. Hale and Gray felt the aircraft shudder as it ran along the uneven ground.

"Reverse engines," said Hale calmly.

Putting the engines in reverse and slowly throttling up, the men slowed the aircraft to a taxi speed.

"I'll turn the plane around, while you open the door."

Gray released his seatbelt and climbed out of the co-pilot's seat. Quickly he ran out of the control cabin and towards the door which was located towards the rear of the fuselage.

"Okay that's it," shouted Curtis over the great roar of the aircraft's four engines. "Thanks again Sergei, are you sure you'll be alright?"

"As soon as you're out of here, we'll disappear," said the Russian.

"Now get moving."

Curtis shook the hand of his old friend, and then ran towards the awaiting aircraft.

"Everything okay, Steve?" asked Gray, as the agent approached.

"Yeah everything's fine," said Curtis as he was helped into the aircraft. "Just get me back to the C.I.A headquarters as fast as you can."

Gray raced back to the cockpit, while Curtis took a rear seat position. The roar of the four engines increased as Captain Hale opened the throttle. The dust cloud became intense as the mighty aircraft roared along the landscape. Slowly the nose of the plane lifted and Curtis was on his way back to the USA.

The rebels listened as the sound of the aircraft diminished into the night sky and Tarelkin wondered what the American scientists would make of the strange object on the moon.

"What now, Sergei?" asked Dezhurov.

"What now? That's up to the Americans."

chapter two
SECRETS REVEALED

October 30th, 1963

An Alouette type helicopter begins to descend over the sun soaked plains of Arizona. Two C.I.A men sit quietly behind the pilot, each one lost in his own thoughts. Agent Steve Curtis looked down at the dry terrain below. It reminded him of the Kazakhstan landscape where, six months before, he had received photographs and information about an amazing discovery on the moon. He and his colleagues at the C.I.A headquarters in Langley Virginia have heard nothing more about this episode until now. Curtis and his C.I.A chief James Hoffman, have been asked to attend a meeting at the top-secret government base at Groom Lake known as Area 51. The meeting has been called by the American industrialist Vigo Saltzman, the chairman of Saltzman aerospace. His company, consisting of eight major industrial complexes around the United States, is responsible for developing the latest military aircraft for the U.S and NATO.

Saltzman is prepared to stop at nothing to keep ahead of every other major company in the world, even if it means stealing someone else's ideas. Descending over the base, Curtis noticed several buildings that resembled aircraft hangars, and many smaller buildings scattered around the area. As the aircraft gently landed inside the perimeter fence, a black

Lincoln continental limousine began to move slowly towards the end of the aircraft runway and stopped within fifty feet of the helicopter. As the aircrafts engines died down, Curtis opened the door and climbed out followed by Hoffman. Throwing their jackets over their shoulders, they walked briskly to the waiting car. A small grey-haired sixty year old man climbed out of the front passenger side of the vehicle and held out his hand to welcome both of them. "Good day gentlemen, my name's Collins," said the man as he shook hands with Curtis and Hoffman. "Mr Saltzman has sent me to meet you, so, if you'd like to take a seat, we'll drive you the short distance to the meeting."

As the two men climbed into the back seat of the Lincoln, Collins closed the door then took his seat at the front of the car.

"Drive on," he said. And the driver of the Lincoln started the engine and quickly had the limousine heading towards the west side of the base.

"Saltzman certainly travels in style," said Hoffman quietly.

"Do you know much about this man Saltzman, Jim?" said Curtis.

"I know of him, but I've never met him till now," replied Hoffman. "What I do know is that his company is responsible for most of our military hard ware, and that gives him a lot of privilege."

Curtis smiled, knowing full well what his boss meant. Privileges by working for the government usually meant you could bend the rules which most people would never be allowed to get away with.

As they were driven across the base, Curtis noticed how the aircraft hangars were heavily guarded. There were machines being hidden from the rest of the world he thought, but what their technology consisted of was kept secret, even to President Kennedy.

The Lincoln came to a halt outside a small office building. An armed security guard approached the vehicle as Collins wound down the window. He reached into his inside pocket and withdrew his security pass. Showing the pass to the guard he said, "It's okay Sergeant these people are expected."

"Thank you, sir, carry on," said the guard as he stepped back from the car.

"Gentlemen, would you like to follow me," said Collins climbing out of the Lincoln. He opened the rear door and Hoffman and Curtis climbed out into the hot midday sun.

"This way please," continued Collins with his butler style approach to his work.

Hoffman and Curtis followed Collins along the concrete path to the main door. Curtis stopped and turned round, glancing across the base, hoping to see something of interest.

"You won't see anything from there my friend," came the sinister voice of the second security guard standing near the entrance. "Can I suggest you move along inside, sir?"

The security guard glared straight into Curtis's eyes as he spoke. Curtis stared back for a moment, but then realized this was not the time for any confrontation. The security guard was only doing his job after all, and they were both supposed to be on the same side.

Curtis walked into the reception area, where Collins and Hoffman were talking to a young woman seated behind a reception desk. She'd been typing most of the morning, so a break from the continual pounding of the keys was quite welcoming.

"I take it you're Mr Curtis?" she said, politely smiling at the agent.

"Yes that's right."

"Would you please wear this identification badge at all times? This is a top security base and you could be stopped by a security guard at any time."

She handed Curtis and Hoffman their badges which were about the same size as a credit card. Both men pinned the badges to their shirt pockets and began to follow Collins. The three of them walked to the end of the room where an elevator was situated. Collins pressed the button to call the lift. "Just one moment, gentlemen and the elevator will be with us."

Curtis could hear the elevator car approaching. With a gentle thud the car stopped and the doors slid open.

"Right gentlemen," said Collins. "If you'd like to press the red button the elevator will take you to the conference room where Mr Saltzman will be waiting for you."

"Thank you," said Hoffman as he and Curtis walked into the elevator car. Hoffman pressed the red button and the doors quietly closed. The elevator began to descend to an underground conference room. While they were waiting for their short journey to end, Curtis looked at Hoffman's identity card.

"How did they manage to obtain our photographs for these cards, chief?"

"I was just thinking that myself. Still, that's not my concern at the moment. Let's find out what this is all about."

The elevator came to a gentle stop and the doors slid open. Both men took a few steps into the room, stopped and looked around.

"This is a conference room?" asked Curtis. "It's better than my living room at home."

The room was about thirty feet square, and covered in a thick dark blue carpet. Hundreds of books on aircraft and engineering filled a huge bookcase which stretched the total distance of the left-hand wall.

Three large sofas each with their own small drinks table were arranged in a rectangle at the centre of the room. Against the wall in a teak cabinet was the latest twenty four inch colour TV, and a cocktail bar which filled the right hand corner of the room. A man in his mid-fifties walked across the room towards them. He was about five foot six inches tall and about one hundred and sixty eight pounds. His hair was completely grey and combed back.

"Gentlemen, come in. I'm Vigo Saltzman and it's nice to meet you both," he said as he shook hands with the C.I.A chief.

"You're Mr Hoffman I take it?"

"Yes, that's right."

"And you're Steve Curtis?"

"Yes, pleased to meet you," said the agent shaking Saltzman's hand. "This is quite a place you have here. It's nice to see were the taxpayers' money is spent."

Saltzman laughed. "Oh, I can assure you, Mr Curtis, what you see here belongs to me. I do insist on having my own home comforts in the workplace. It makes coming to work more enjoyable, wouldn't you agree?"

"I wouldn't know," said Curtis. "I'm usually out in the field being shot at by the enemy."

"I know all about that, Mr Curtis, please forgive me. Now let me get both of you a drink."

They followed Saltzman across the room to the cocktail bar where two other men who had arrived much earlier were sipping at their whisky. They were military men dressed in full uniform, a U.S army colonel in his late sixties, and a young U.S air force captain in his early thirties.

"Right, Mr Hoffman, I understand you like your whisky neat, is that right?" asked Saltzman.

"Yes, that's fine thank you."

"And you, Mr Curtis, a Martini?"

"Thank you," said the agent.

Curtis was well aware of secrecy in his business, but he felt uncomfortable. Saltzman had obtained photographs of himself and Hoffman for their identity cards without their knowledge, now he knew what both of them liked to drink. What else did he know about the two

C.I.A officers? Curtis felt it best to cooperate with this man for the time being, but also to tread carefully and not give too much away. Saltzman walked from behind the bar and handed the drinks to Hoffman and Curtis.

"There you go gentlemen. Now can I introduce you all? First we have Colonel John Gorman of the United States army, and flight Lieutenant Dave Rossi of the American air force. Mr Rossi is training with N.A.S.A at the moment for one of their Apollo missions."

"Nice to meet you Lieutenant," said Curtis shaking Rossi's hand. "If I wasn't with the C.I.A I wouldn't have minded joining N.A.S.A myself."

Rossi smiled. "Well, there are times when I wonder what the hell I've got myself into, but I think I'll get there."

"I don't think we've met, Colonel," said Hoffman. "What army division are you with at the moment?"

"I'm not with a division, Mr Hoffman. I'm serving with another group at present."

Gorman and Saltzman looked at each other but said nothing.

"Now gentlemen, may I suggest that we all sit down and make ourselves comfortable," said the industrialist, in an attempt to stop any more questions.

The four men walked across the room to the three couches and sat themselves down, while Saltzman crossed to a section of the bookcase.

From between two encyclopaedias he withdrew a large envelope. "Now gentlemen, I want you to take a look at these photographs," he said handing out three copies to each to the four men. Curtis immediately recognised that they were similar to the prints given to him by Tarelkin six months earlier. They were photographs of the Sinus Medii region of the moon, but better quality with the object more prominent.

"Recognise them, Mr Curtis?" asked Saltzman.

"Yes, I see you've improved on them."

"What are we looking at, Vigo?" asked Gorman.

The army colonel sounded quite intimidating. He had a voice to match his six foot four appearance. It was big and powerful enough to scare the life out of anyone serving under him.

"Six months ago Colonel, Mr Curtis received from his contact in Russia a set of photographs similar to the ones you have in front of you. When they came into our possession it was decided that we would construct and send our own space probe to investigate. Our camera lenses are much better than the ones the Russians use, and we used a special film made by Kodak Eastman. As you say, Mr Curtis, we have improved on the image."

"This contact of yours Curtis, I take it he's Russian?" said Gorman.

"Yes, he's Russian."

"Can he be trusted?"

Curtis paused for a moment, his eyes fixed on Gorman. "Yes he can be trusted."

"How do we know?"

"Because I said so," replied the C.I.A man.

"Gentlemen," said Saltzman. "I appreciate we know very little about one another, but I feel that if we are to achieve our objective we must trust each other, agreed?"

"Agreed," said Curtis glaring at Gorman.

Saltzman realised there could be some friction between the two C.I.A agents and the military men. It was imperative to him that he reduced the tension the best he could.

Hoffman turned to look at Curtis and whispered to his colleague. "We have to play along for the moment, Steve, if we're to find out what this is about."

Saltzman began to prance back and forth like an expectant father. This is how he liked to be in control. Employees seated, with him standing over them. It gave him a sense of superiority over the people he worked with.

"Now gentlemen, as I was saying, we constructed our own space probe from scratch. The vehicle was designed by my own company and launched from this very base."

"Did N.A.S.A know about it?" asked Hoffman.

Saltzman paused, and looked at Gorman. "No they didn't."

"Why not?"

Saltzman looked uneasy as he answered. "Well it was thought that the mission should be kept secret."

"Who decided it should be kept a secret?" pressed the chief of the C.I.A. "Who's in charge of this operation?"

"Maybe we should allow Vigo to finish what he's saying, then maybe we'll all be a little wiser," said Gorman, interrupting Hoffman's questions.

"As you said chief, let's play along," whispered Curtis.

"Carry on Vigo," said Gorman.

Saltzman continued, "Using our own radars here at Area 51 we were able to track the vehicle around the moon as it photographed its target area.

When the images were transmitted back to us we processed them in our laboratories.

We believe the Russians are right when they say they think it could be an alien spacecraft."

"Alien spacecraft," exclaimed Rossi. "Are you serious?"

There was silence amongst the group as all of them scrutinised the prints in front of them.

"How sure are we on this Vigo?" asked Gorman.

"Well from the way it shines it certainly looks metallic."

Gorman looked hard at the prints. "Any idea how long it's been there?"

"That we don't know, but we intend to find out," said the industrialist with great excitement.

Hoffman wasn't convinced. "Now listen Saltzman, the C.I.A have been investigating UFO incidents for some time now and I think the whole thing is pure nonsense. I don't know what that thing is, but there could be a hundred and one explanations for it."

"But I believe there is only one Mr Hoffman."

Saltzman began to prance back and forth once more.

"For the first time in the history of mankind the two most powerful nations on this planet are setting out on the greatest voyage of all. A voyage to the stars, gentlemen."

Saltzman spoke with great enthusiasm, as if the space programme had been started just for him. He continued, "When it comes to conquering the universe we are nothing more than a child taking its first footsteps. Yet we will do it, oh yes my friends. We'll do it."

Once more there was silence in the room as Saltzman walked towards Gorman. He sat down next to him and began to talk softly. "Gentleman, tell me, has it ever occurred to you that while we are on this voyage of discovery we just might stumble across artefacts left by another race of beings. Technology years more advanced than ours, just think of it, if we could reach it."

"Yes, I can think of it," said Hoffman. "I can think of how dangerous mankind would become with technology he couldn't understand. That's if you believe in aliens in the first place."

"Oh they exist, Mr Hoffman," said Saltzman. "I'd like you to hear Colonel Gorman's story, then I'll show you something. Is that alright with you Colonel?"

"I've no problem with that, if Mr Hoffman, Mr Curtis and the Lieutenant wish to hear it."

Hoffman shrugged his shoulders. "Go ahead,"

Gorman sat up straight, took a deep breath and began to tell his story.

"Well, after the battle of Britain was fought, the German plan to invade the United Kingdom was cancelled. Hitler then gave top priority to the development of the V weapons.

Under the leadership of their top rocket scientist, Werner Von Braun, who successfully developed and test fired a V2 rocket in 1942, the Germans as we know from history began to mass produce and perfect these rockets. Now, after the allies invaded Europe, I was given orders to take one hundred men north to the Baltic coast. Our mission was to penetrate the German rocket base at Peenemunde and steal as much rocket technology as possible. What we didn't know at the time was that the Russians had the same plan. Once we received the news of the advancing Soviet army, we took as much as we could and destroyed the rest."

"What's this got to do with our object on the moon?" asked Hoffman.

"Well, Mr Hoffman, after the war the rocket components were taken to the United States. A missile base was set up at White Sands in New Mexico with Von Braun as head of the rocket team. By the mid nineteen forties we were test firing our own rockets and equipping them with film cameras. For the first time our scientists could see our planet from space. We began to look at the curvature of the earth, the thin atmosphere that surrounds it and the delicate balance of life itself.

We felt that looking at our own world first would help us in the future when we set our sights on other planets. The conquest of space excited all of us. I have to say it was the most thrilling time of my career to be at the start of our country's space programme."

Gorman paused for a moment and took a sip of whisky before continuing his story.

"It was the night of January 10th 1947 when it happened. I was overseeing our rocket programme at White Sands. A thunderstorm swept across most of the state so all our aircraft were grounded. Lieutenant Alan Truman, our radar operator was at his post checking for enemy aircraft.

There was always a chance of a Russian spy plane flying overhead so security was always at maximum. The Lieutenant then asked Sergeant Peter Davis and myself to look at something on his radar scope."

January 10th, 1947

Gorman and Davis were standing in the corner of the radar room talking about the day's events when Lieutenant Truman called out.

"Sir, I have a blip on my scope that I think you ought to see."

Both officers walked quickly towards Truman.

"What is it?" asked Davis.

"I have an object on my scope, sir, coming in from the northwest. Its speed, it's unbelievable, it's at least Mach four."

"Check it," said Gorman quietly to Davis.

The Sergeant had been a radar operator himself on joining the air force, and Gorman wanted a second opinion. Davis leant forward towards the radar scope. The blip was indeed moving faster than any aircraft the Americans had, and as far as Davis knew, anything the Russians possessed.

"He's right, sir," said a worried Davis. "It can't be ours."

"Russian?" asked Gorman.

"No, I don't think so."

The three men watched the scope and waited.

"Height ten thousand feet, losing speed rapidly, now Mach one and decreasing."

"What's its heading, lieutenant?" asked Gorman.

Truman swivelled around in his chair and looked straight at the Colonel.

"It's heading our way, sir, and at that speed it will be here in approximately five minutes."

"Okay let's go to red alert Sergeant. I don't know what that thing is but we have to assume that it's hostile. Are you sure the 509TH have nothing flying?"

"I'm sure, sir, everything's grounded because of the weather."

"Colonel, wait," shouted Truman. The radar operator looked hard at the scope. The tiny blip was almost stationary. "It's coming down, sir, it must be in trouble."

Truman grabbed a pen and pad from the side of his desk, and started to write down the craft's trajectory telemetry. As he watched he saw the blip on his scope disappear.

"It's down Colonel. It's only about twenty miles north of this base."

"Right we need to find that craft before anyone else," said Gorman.

"Sergeant, get together a group of about ten men. If we're on to something, the fewer people who know about this the better."

"Okay, sir, I'm on it."

"Also get some transport vehicles and heavy lifting equipment. Whatever this is we have to capture it."

"Yes, sir."

Davis immediately left the radar room to follow Gorman's orders.

As he began to run down the corridor, two army engineers, Privates Paul Kidman and Charles Murray, entered the building.

"Kidman, Murray," called out Davis. "I want you to come with me."

"What's wrong, sir?" asked Kidman.

Davis had no time to explain. "Kidman do we have lifting equipment to raise a fighter aircraft out of the ground?"

"Yes, sir, why? Have one of our guys come down?"

"Possibly." Davis knew it could be something much bigger than any of them realised, but he thought it better to say as little as possible for the moment.

"Look, I want you go and get that equipment and meet me and

Colonel Gorman outside this building in five minutes. I've got to round up some other men."

"Yes, sir."

Meanwhile Gorman had returned to his office. He quickly slipped on a large overcoat and walked over to the window. Pealing back the curtain he looked out into the darkness.

"Thank god for the bad weather," he thought. "With a bit of luck this heavy rain should keep people indoors."

He made his way out of his office and down the corridor to the exit door. Davis had assembled a team of engineers and was waiting for the Colonel.

"We're ready, sir," said Davis as Gorman approached the group.

"Good, have you told the men what the situation is?"

"No, sir."

"Right leave this to me." Gorman turned to the engineers.

"Just gather round will you."

The eight engineers formed a small semi-circle around Gorman and listened carefully.

"Gentlemen, ten minutes ago an unidentified aircraft was picked up on our radar. It's believed that the vehicle has landed or crashed twenty miles north of this area. Our job is to recover it and bring it back to this base. Now we have no idea of the craft's origin so secrecy must be obtained at all time, is that clear?"

"Yes, sir," said all eight engineers simultaneously.

"Right, let's go."

Gorman and Davis led the team outside. As the rain lashed down, the headlights from two military vehicles could be seen approaching the radar centre. They both came to a halt opposite the main door way. The first one, driven by Private Kidman, was a large army wagon for carrying the engineers. The second vehicle, driven by Murray, had a long trailer with a small crane fixed to the end nearest the cab which was used for lifting and carrying sections of aircraft or machinery from one air base to the next.

"Right, in the back of the first truck all of you," ordered Davis.

The eight men ran to the rear of the vehicle. Each one took it in turn to hoist himself into the back of the truck, while Gorman and Davis climbed into the cab next to Kidman.

"Okay, let's go," said Gorman.

Both vehicles began to move away from the building, their windscreen wipers on maximum speed as the rain caused poor visibility to both drivers.

"Sir, have you given any thought to what this craft could be?"

Gorman looked at Davis. "I'm not sure what it is. What I do know is that we have to find that thing tonight."

"What about the men with us. What if we find something that doesn't belong to any country?"

"Let's find it first, we'll worry about where it comes from later."

Davis was concerned about what his men would find. He thought about the interrogation that all of them may be subjected to by government authorities if the craft were extraterrestrial.

Saltzman, Hoffman, Curtis and Rossi continued to listen with great interest to Gorman's story.

"What did you find?" asked Curtis.

"Well, we continued driving for at least an hour, then Kidman noticed something about two hundred yards from the roadside."

"Jesus, Colonel. Look at that!"

The three men looked east of the main road. Lying at a twenty degree angle lay a silver metallic elliptical disk-shaped object about forty feet in diameter. A small section had been torn away as the craft had hit the ground, but the rest of the vehicle was in one piece.

"Get over there Kidman, quick," shouted Davis.

The Private steered the truck off the road and onto the rugged New Mexico terrain. The eight engineers in the back of the vehicle were rocked back and forth as the driver headed towards the crashed aircraft.

"Wait, stop the truck," said Gorman.

Kidman slowed the army vehicle down bringing it to a halt fifty yards away from the disk. The three men sat motionless as they stared at the unearthly machine.

"Sergeant, you and the men stay here," said Gorman as he glared at a craft that he realized was not of this earth. He climbed out of the truck and cautiously walked towards the object. He had never seen anything like this in his military career. He felt a strange kind of fear come over him which he had never experienced in the whole of his life. It was obvious to the colonel that the craft was extraterrestrial, the thing was, what was his next move? He didn't know whether it was curiosity or stupidity that drove him towards the machine, but he had to find out more about it. He stopped within a few feet of the craft and stared at it glistening in the truck's headlights as rain ran down its metallic skin. He walked over to the damaged section and slowly and cautiously looked inside. He climbed slowly into the torn section, and began working himself upwards into the interior of the machine. The craft's metal was no thicker than tinfoil, yet was capable of taking Gorman's full weight without distorting. As he marvelled at the strength of the machine's material, he realized it must have been a terrific impact to have damaged this craft. Looking up he noticed a hole in what he thought could be the floor of the flight deck.

"I can get through there," he thought.

Nervously he slid his head through the hole and began to look around. He could see what looked like a control panel. It was about six feet long and three feet high. In front of it were two small seats which looked only big enough to accommodate children. Gorman slowly turned his head away from the control console. Suddenly he froze. Lying motionless on the floor about ten feet away from the control panel was the spacecraft's pilot.

He wore a white jumpsuit made from a silk material, with footwear resembling children's plimsolls, which were made from blue fabric. His hands were humanoid, with four fingers and a thumb, but they were small like a child's hand. From the angle that he was laying on the flight deck floor, it wasn't possible for Gorman to see the pilot's face. He could see the top of his head however which was covered in thick blonde hair. Sadly there was no movement or any sign of breathing and Gorman realized that recovering a live alien was unlikely.

Knowing he had to move quickly while still keeping the whole episode secret, Gorman slowly climbed down through the twisted metal and back into the open. It had stopped raining now which would help in recovering the craft and its occupant. He walked quickly towards the army vehicle. Davis climbed out of the cab and ran to meet his superior officer, eager to find out what Gorman had seen.

"Well, sir?" he asked.

"Davis, get the men and the lifting equipment over here as fast as you can, we don't have much time."

"Yes, I'll do that. Is there anything else you want to tell me, Colonel?" asked Davis, hoping Gorman would reveal a little more about the craft.

"Just get this thing on the back of that transporter, Sergeant. We've got to get this craft back to our base as soon as possible. Once we've loaded it up I want each and every man to collect every piece of wreckage within a hundred yards radius no matter how small."

In the underground conference room at Area 51 Steve Curtis and the rest of the group continued to listen to Gorman's story.

"Colonel how many of the engineers realized you'd found an alien craft?" said Curtis.

"All of them. Those men behaved with great professionalism. I was proud of them all. It was obvious to them the vehicle was extraterrestrial and security would have to be given top priority."

"What about the alien?" asked Rossi.

"I don't know what happened to him. In fact after two days I never saw the spacecraft again either. We arrived back at the base just as the sun began to rise and the alien craft was taken to one of our large aircraft hangars. The storm cleared by morning and I remember gazing out of my office window across the base to the hangar housing the spacecraft. At first I wasn't sure what to do. Was I to tell my military superiors, or report the incident to the president?

Apart from the team, Sergeant Davis and I myself we were the only people who knew the craft was extraterrestrial. Everyone else on the base had been told that it was a top-secret aircraft and that they were to keep well away from the hangar. I thought our secret was safe until Davis came to my office."

"Colonel, I have to see you straightaway, sir."

"Yes Sergeant, what is it?"

"I've just had word that two teenagers claim to have seen a huge fireball in the sky when they were on their way home last night."

Gorman quickly walked to his desk and picked up his telephone.

"Do we know their names?"

"Yes, sir," said Davis looking down at the notepad in his left hand.

"They're Bobby Carter and his girlfriend Pamela Sue Jenkins, both aged nineteen."

"Get me General Glenn at Fort Worth Texas, priority call please," said Gorman with great urgency in his voice. "Have they told anyone?

"I'm afraid so, sir. They've told the local radio station and the newspaper people are crawling all over them."

"General Glenn?" said Gorman. "This is Colonel John Gorman, sir, at

White Sands. We have an emergency situation, sir, concerning a crashed vehicle that we recovered in the early hours of this morning."

There was a short pause as Gorman listened to the general's reply.

"Yes, we believe that's possible General, but the main problem is that the local radio station and media have had the incident reported to them."

Davis sensed concern, but certainly no panic in Gorman's voice. His years of experience in army combat and making split second decisions was nothing new to the Colonel. Now his military judgment was being put to the ultimate test, as the security of the United States and maybe the entire world was now resting on his decisions.

"Yes, sir, I'll do that immediately," said Gorman. He replaced the telephone and walked towards Davis. "Sergeant, we have to move everything from this base immediately."

"Everything, sir, where to?"

"Wright Paterson airbase, so let's get moving."

Gorman headed towards the door followed by Davis. They emerged into the bright desert sunlight and headed towards the hangar.

"Colonel, why are we moving everything to Wright airbase?"

"Because Sergeant, Wright air base is where the foreign technology department is based. Their job is to reverse engineer any technology that comes into their possession. That means they find out how it works, then reproduce it for our country's use. I understand the Russians have a similar department. It's what's known as keeping the balance of power between us. The trick is to keep one step ahead of the other guy so we always have the edge."

As they walked briskly across the base, Gorman turned to Davis. "Crazy isn't it, we, the Russians, and the British spend millions developing weapons only for each of us to cancel one another out."

"I'm afraid it's the way we've all become, sir, paranoid. It's destroying us all. Do I take it they're going to try to discover the technology behind this craft?"

"Looks like it, let's hope the Russians don't have one of these in their possession."

As both men entered the hangar, they walked towards the alien spacecraft, saluting the other officers as they passed them. Gorman suddenly stopped and stared at the strange space vehicle.

"Something wrong Colonel?" asked Davis.

"Do you know, I've heard people talk about these things so many times, but I could never believe any of it until now?"

"I know how you feel, sir, but the fact is it's here and it's in our control."

"Yes it's here all right. The question is, why?"

"Colonel, what if they're hostile?"

"That has occurred to me. A race that is obviously technically superior to us would have no problem launching a full scale attack and defeating us in a matter of days."

Gorman walked towards the spacecraft leaving Davis to think about what he'd just said. As he reached the alien machine, he turned to address the engineers working around him.

The engineers immediately stopped what they were doing and approached Gorman, forming a semi-circle around him.

"Right listen up. We've been given orders to transport this vehicle to Wright Paterson airbase for further examination. I want you to pack every piece of metal, no matter how small or insignificant you may think it is, into sealed containers. I want everything we've got on board our transport plane by fourteen hundred hours. Carry on."

Without any questions the engineers began to carry out Gorman's orders. Davis approached the Colonel with a look of great concern on his face.

"Sir," said Davis. "There are a large number of people who have seen this spacecraft. What's going to happen to them?"

"What do you mean?"

Davis paused for a moment. "Colonel, I'm concerned about security. If just one of these people should talk or speak out of line, who knows what the consequences could be."

"Alright, I understand what you're saying, but at the moment our main concern is to get everything out of here. Now, is the alien still in the medical centre?"

"Yes, sir, no autopsy can be performed until we get clearance."

"Right, this is what I want you to do. First of all that spacecraft is to be covered up before we load it onto the transport plane.

Use covers, sheets, anything, just prevent as many people as possible from seeing that thing. Once you've done that, pack the alien in an ice filled casket and make sure it's locked."

"Yes, sir, I'll do that."

"Carry on," said Gorman.

Davis saluted his superior officer then went to supervise the Colonel's orders. Gorman stood at the doorway of the hangar. He turned to look at the alien craft for the last time.

"My God, the whole world's about to change because of this," he thought.

As Gorman finished his story, it was obvious that there were more questions the group wanted answers to.

"Once the spacecraft and alien arrived at Wright Paterson airbase, who took control of the situation?" asked Hoffman.

"I don't know," replied Gorman. "Once we arrived it was taken out of my hands. We reported to General Glenn who had arrived at the base two hours earlier. We gave him our report then we were told not to talk to anyone about the incident. We were even ordered not to talk amongst ourselves about what we had found in case anyone overheard."

"Weren't you curious about what happened to the spacecraft and its pilot?"

"Sure we were curious, but we were military. We knew how to take orders."

Rossi, who had been writing notes on a small pad as Gorman told his story, leant forward in the seat.

"What happened to the engineers who recovered the alien craft?"

"Immediately after the incident the entire unit was separated and stationed in different bases around the world. Peter Davis was stationed at a base in West Germany but I could never find out which one."

"And I take it you haven't seen the spacecraft since that day, is that right?" asked Curtis.

"Oh, I have seen the spacecraft several times, isn't that right, Vigo?"

"That's right," said Saltzman in a loud voice. He stood up and walked across the room towards his desk.

He opened the top right hand drawer and inside, hidden under a notepad, was a metal plate about two inches square with a red button in the centre.

Saltzman pressed the button then slowly closed the drawer. A slight humming sound came from the bookcase which drew the attention of the group. Suddenly a large section began to slide to one side revealing a door behind it.

"Gentlemen, if you'd like to follow me," said Saltzman making his way towards the door.

Curtis, Hoffman, Gorman and Rossi followed him down a corridor about fifty feet in length which led into an underground aircraft hangar. As they entered Curtis noticed there were no military personnel. A slight rumbling of the air conditioning was the only sound that could be heard. The entire place was as clean as a hospital surgery, with a floor so highly polished,

Curtis could see his reflection. Saltzman walked past the group and stopped just in front of them, then pointed towards the centre of the hangar.

"There you have it gentlemen,"

The group turned and looked, their eyes wide in disbelief. There, standing in the centre of the hangar, stood the spacecraft which Gorman and the engineers had retrieved from the New Mexico desert January the 10th 1947. Saltzman approached Gorman.

"Colonel?" he said holding out his hand towards the craft, inviting Gorman to take another look at the space vehicle. Gorman began to walk towards the machine. In his own personal way he was pleased to see the spacecraft again. After all, it was he who discovered it, and he was the first man, as far as he knew, to look upon a being from another world. It was as if the alien vehicle belonged to him. Hoffman approached Saltzman.

"How long have you had this in your possession?" he said in disbelief at what he saw in front of him.

"Since they brought it from Wright airbase in 1947, Mr Hoffman. Would you like to take a look?"

Saltzman walked towards the spacecraft, followed by Hoffman, Curtis and Rossi. Meanwhile Gorman was studying the vehicle like he did the night he'd discovered it. The metallic skin still shone just like it did sixteen years before. There was no sign of rust, oxidisation or any ageing of the metal. Gorman felt drawn to the section of the craft that had been torn away in the crash. It brought back memories of the night he climbed through the twisted metal and discovered the alien's body.

"You know, every time I come here to look at this craft I get goose bumps, Vigo."

"Yes I think I understand," replied Saltzman.

Although Gorman had been to area 51 many time to look at the craft, he couldn't help being drawn to the spaceship and gently touching it with the tips of his fingers.

"I'm interested to know what you've discovered about this craft in the past sixteen years, if that's possible," said Hoffman.

The head of the C.I.A had never believed in aliens before this moment, so now he wanted to know everything. Just then the sound of footsteps came from the far side of the hangar. A tall grey-haired man in his seventies, wearing a white overall similar to a doctor's, approached.

"Good day, Professor," said Saltzman.

"Good day, Mr Saltzman," replied the man with a thick German accent.

"Gentlemen, may I introduce you to Professor Gerhard Steiner. The professor has been working on this project for the past ten years. He came to live in our country after the Second World War, and was one of the rocket scientists who worked with Werner Von Braun before he was assigned to us."

"You mean he was a Nazi?" said Curtis.

The room went quiet for a moment.

"That was a long time ago, Mr Curtis," said Steiner. "Those are days we're not proud of, and some of us wish to forget."

"You better hope we don't forget them professor. The day we do will be the day it happens all over again." Curtis then turned and walked towards the spacecraft.

"Don't take it personally professor," said Hoffman quietly.

"Steve's seen enough war to last him a life time."

Steiner looked directly at the C.I.A chief and said, "You think he has bad memories, I'll have you know, Mr Hoffman, I lost most of my family at the hands of the Gestapo, until I agreed to work for them. If you were a scientist like me, then you were forced to work for the third Reich. Don't think for one minute that all Germans were willing supporters of Hitler."

"Gentlemen, why don't we look at the spacecraft in more detail," said Saltzman.

He was eager that the group examine the craft and ask as many questions as they wished. He would need their help in the future for his own interests of course, so it was important that he tried to maintain a good relationship with each one of them.

"Now, Mr Curtis, I'm sure you and the others would like to know what we've discovered," he said, as he approached the American agent.

"Yes, I would. I'd be interested to know about their form of propulsion."

"Professor, would you like to explain?" asked Saltzman.

Steiner approached the spaceship and began to describe the vehicle's mechanisms.

"Well gentlemen, we've discovered that the space vehicle runs on nothing more than electrical and magnetic power."

"Is it nuclear?" asked Rossi.

"No Lieutenant, it's not even nuclear. It's just ordinary electrical power. The aliens know how to use their resources better than we do of course, but nevertheless it's electric."

"So how does it work?" asked Rossi.

"There is a round electrical coil, six inches in diameter, running around the circumference of the spacecraft. Below the coil is a cleverly designed lattice grid which is covered in an advanced form of metal not found on Earth. I think that would be the best way to describe it, wouldn't you say, Mr Saltzman? Once the current starts to travel through the coil, ion energy is created in the space between the grid and the coil. It is this ion energy that causes the spacecraft to lift off the ground at great velocity."

"What happens when it reaches space?" asked Curtis.

"Once it reaches space, Mr Curtis, the aliens use a sophisticated magnetic drive to propel themselves through outer space."

"You mean, they travelled possible millions of miles in this tiny craft?" asked Hoffman.

"I don't think so, Mr Hoffman," said Steiner. "It's my belief this vehicle would rendezvous with a much larger mother ship for the great journey across the galaxy, but it could travel to the moon and back without any problem."

"I take it no one knows about this vehicle, only you people?" said Hoffman. He felt there was more to all of this and he wanted to know what it was and who was behind Saltzman.

"Well, there is another group that know of the spacecraft's existence, isn't that right Colonel?"

"Yes there is. Have you heard of Majestic, Mr Hoffman?"

"Yes I've heard of them. A group specially set up to investigate UFO encounters."

"That's right. Earlier today you asked who was in charge of this operation, didn't you?"

"Yes I did and now I know….you are. You're part of Majestic, aren't you?"

"That's right."

It was now clear to Hoffman and Curtis who was running this operation, and it wasn't the president. It was a group separate from the government with rules of their own not even Kennedy or Hoffman could challenge.

"And I have no doubt everything you find is kept to yourselves?"

"That's not true," said Saltzman. "We disclose technical information to the N.A.S.A. scientists as we find it."

"What about the technical information you don't want N.A.S.A. to know about?" asked Curtis.

"There's technical information that has to remain a secret for the security of our country, Mr Curtis, you people should know that," replied Gorman.

"Ah yes, national security. They've become convenient words to enable people like you to keep things to yourself, right Colonel?"

"Gentlemen, please, we're getting nowhere like this," said Saltzman. He could see friction beginning to take root within the group and it was important to keep these people together if he was to ensure keeping his plans on track. "Look I know we are going to have a difference of opinion a times, but please it's for the best that we work together, trust me. Now would you like to follow me and the professor, we've something else we want to show you."

Hoffman and Curtis stood and looked at one another for a moment, but neither of them said anything. Saltzman and Majestic had in their possession a spacecraft, which to Hoffman more important people should have been made aware of. It was obvious to the CIA boss that Saltzman aerospace could not be allowed to monopolise everything the alien craft had to offer.

The group followed Saltzman and Steiner around to the other side of the spacecraft. The small control consul had been removed from inside the spaceship and placed on the hangar floor. A one inch power cable had been connected to the rear of the consul.

This led across the hangar floor to a generator situated at the far side of the underground building.

"Right gentlemen, this is the control consul we removed from the spacecraft," said Steiner. "We discovered that its electrical power is identical to ours on earth, thus making it easy for us to activate it. We removed a circuit board from inside the consul for examination, and we noticed there were no transistors or components similar to what we use."

The professor picked up the circuit board and rested it on the consul. He took a pen from his inside pocket and began to point out the tiny square and rectangular shaped chips inserted into the board.

"Gentlemen would you like to take a closer look at these little black square chips?"

The five men gathered round the professor and peered at the advanced circuit board.

"These chips that you are looking at hold more electronic information than any of our largest computers."

"What are they made of?" asked Hoffman.

"They're made of silicon."

"Silicon?" replied a surprised Rossi.

"Yes Lieutenant, you're amazed and you have every right to be. Silicon is an insulator, but anything that's computerized or uses radio waves depends on semi-conductors. What the aliens have done is to allow charged particles to move freely in the silicon by adding certain elements to it."

"How have they done it?" asked Gorman.

"We think there are several layers to each chip. One of the layers is a thin coating of metal which is etched away in order to contain the transistors. It really is an ingenious piece of technology. It means that computers can be made many times smaller than the ones we have today."

"Can we copy it?" asked Hoffman.

"In time, Mr Hoffman."

Curtis began to look at the small red control consul, with the two tiny black leather seats in front of it. There were two vertical rows of buttons running down the left side of the consul, about fifty in total. Each button was half an inch square, white in colour and had some sort of hieroglyphic marking in the centre.

"Have you made out what that means?" asked Curtis pointing to one of them.

"It's obviously some form of lettering," said the professor.

"We'd like to decode it but unfortunately there's not enough of the lettering to enable us to work out any form of alphabet."

Curtis looked at the centre of the consul which had a large black screen in the centre.

"I take it this screen gives some form of TV transmission?"

"No, Mr Curtis, it's a liquid crystal display screen."

"Liquid crystal display, what the hell's that?" asked Rossi.

"Well lieutenant, you notice that there are no dials, alter meters, artificial horizon, or any form of instrumentation like you would find in one of our aircraft, is there?"

"No, there isn't."

"That's because all the information about the spacecraft, like speed, attitude, etcetera, is displayed on this screen. Mr Saltzman, could you switch on the main power supply please?"

Saltzman followed a power cable leading from the back of the consul towards the mains isolation switch on the wall of the hangar. Throwing the isolator upwards, Saltzman turned towards the group.

"Okay Professor, power on."

Steiner pressed the top left button on the control panel. A faint hum began to emit from the consul and instantly hieroglyphic lettering and numbers filled the screen.

"God, look at that," said Rossi. "How the hell does it work professor?"

"Polarised light, Mr Rossi. There are six layers which make up one display screen. The first screen is a vertical filter film to polarise the light as it enters. Behind this screen is a glass substrate with ITO electrodes. The shapes of these electrodes determine the dark shapes that will appear when the L.C.D is turned on or off and vertical ridges are etched on the surface so

the liquid crystals are in line with the polarised light. The third layer is a twisted liquid crystal placed in front of an electrode film. The fifth layer is a filter that allows the light through and on to the final screen, which reflects the light from its surface back to the viewer."

"My God, that's incredible," muttered Gorman.

"And very practical, Colonel. It means that heavy cathode ray tubes are now obsolete and control panels on aircraft can be made much smaller."

Gorman was impressed. He could see many ways that this technology could be used in defence as well as civilian use.

"Can you copy this technology, professor?" Saltzman laughed.

"We're already ahead of you Colonel. Saltzman Enterprises have already started to produce the liquid crystal display screen."

"Oh, I see. The Saltzman's empire has wasted no time in investing into this technology," said Curtis sarcastically. "That should boost the profits for your shareholders, wouldn't you say?"

"And what about the spacecraft itself. Have you tried to copy that too?" asked Hoffman.

There was a moment's silence. Saltzman's smile quickly disappeared as he looked at Professor Steiner.

"Gentlemen, I think we've seen enough to convince you that extraterrestrial beings have visited our world. Shall we go back to the comfort of my committee room?"

Saltzman walked away from the group, avoiding Hoffman's last question. Each of the men looked at one another, all of them wondering if the industrialist had something to hide. Steiner then began to follow Saltzman with Gorman and Lt Rossi. As Hoffman headed to the committee room, Curtis placed his hand on his chief's shoulder.

"Sir, just a second," whispered Curtis.

"What's wrong?" said Hoffman. He could see something was bothering his C.I.A colleague.

"Have you noticed the pilots' seats next to the control consul?"

"Sure, what's wrong with them?"

"There are two of them. This is a two-man spacecraft. According to Gorman, the night they discovered the craft they found one of the crew inside. If that story's accurate, what happened to the second alien?"

Hoffman looked straight at Curtis but said nothing. Now he realized something was being kept from them. The question was, did Lt Rossi know anything? Did he know more than the C.I.A agents, or were there questions he wanted answering.

"Let's go and join the rest of them Steve," said Hoffman.

"Let's see if we can dig out a little more information."

As Hoffman and Curtis entered the committee room Saltzman and Gorman were standing talking quietly together. Were they talking about the alien craft or something else? Hoffman wasn't sure. He knew Saltzman wanted to involve the C.I.A, but for what purpose?

Rossi sat on one the couches in the centre of the room, studying the four photographs, while Steiner stood at the bookcase reading a dossier which he had written about the alien spacecraft.

"Gentlemen, please sit down," said Saltzman. The two C.I.A men, Gorman, and the professor, joined Rossi in making themselves comfortable as the industrialist stood in front of the group.

"Well, Mr Saltzman," began Hoffman. "Do you have any more surprises for us?"

"Yes, I probably do have more surprises for you. I have no intention of keeping anything secret. Why would I have asked you and Mr Curtis here today if I didn't want you to know what our plans were?"

"Right, we'll get to our involvement later," said Hoffman, sitting forward and looking directly at Saltzman. "First of all does Kennedy know what you have here?"

"Good God no, we don't tell him anything," said Saltzman angrily.

"Well, if it hasn't escaped your notice, he does happen to be the President who runs the country."

"Wrong," said Gorman in a firm voice. "He and his brother think they run the country."

"What are you talking about Gorman?" said Curtis. The C.I.A agent wasn't happy with Gorman and Saltzman's anti Kennedy attitude.

"You know what I mean. He's weak," said Gorman angrily. "We can't let him know about this. It would be taken out of our hands."

"Oh, so that's what you're afraid of?"

"You bet your fucking life that's what I'm afraid of."

The discussion was now getting heated to a point where any co-operation between the C.I.A, Majestic, and Saltzman aerospace would not be able to function. Saltzman couldn't afford to let that happen. He had to try to calm the situation.

"Listen, Mr Hoffman," he said. "There's something we have to tell you."

"Ok," said Hoffman. "Let's hear it."

"You asked a few moments ago if we'd tried to copy the spacecraft."

"And have you?"

"Well soon after we came into possession of the spacecraft, we had enormous pressure put upon us by the government."

"What sort of pressure?"

"We were asked... No, I'll rephrase that, we were ordered to make a copy of that spaceship. We were told to find out how it worked, and then build one just like it."

"Did you succeed?" asked Rossi.

"No, I'm afraid we didn't." Saltzman walked across the room to sit down. He had a glass of whisky which he sipped before carrying on speaking. "In fact it was a terrible disaster. We were given just six months to build and test-fly our disk vehicle. We constructed its shape easily enough, which we made from aluminium, but it was its magnetic drive that we couldn't replicate. So, with time running out, we installed the vehicle with a small rocket engine."

"Did it have a crew?" asked Curtis.

"Yes, it had a two-man crew, both of them test pilots. In the July of 1947 we made our first test flight. The disk vehicle was fixed beneath a B-25 bomber which took off from this base. Flying at an altitude of thirty thousand feet they flew south over a desolate area of New Mexico. The vehicle was then released from its umbilical arms with the two men on board."

Saltzman paused for a moment and took another sip at his whisky. The five men with their eyes fixed on Saltzman could see he looked troubled by this event in the summer of 1947. He took a deep breath and continued.

"The vehicle began a freefall before the two pilots ignited the engine. Once they did, the craft immediately began to spin out of control. With no stabiliser fins or rudder, both men fought desperately to gain some control over the vehicle."

"What happened?" asked Hoffman.

"I'm afraid to say it smashed into the ground at a terrific speed. The vehicle was so hot that a large pool of glass was found two days later, caused by the heat of the craft as it melted the sand across the desert. Wreckage was found for miles, and as for the pilots, well they were just unrecognisable."

"Surely somebody must have found some wreckage and reported it," said Hoffman.

"Reported it, Mr Hoffman?" said Saltzman as he stood up and walked across the room. He stopped and quickly turned round to face the group.

"Why gentlemen, it's the most reported incident ever. Our crashed vehicle was reported on the second of July 1947 by a ranch hand near the town of Roswell."

The group sat shocked when they heard the name of the town.

"I'm sure you have all heard of that place?"

"Roswell?" said Rossi. Are you telling us the UFO incident at Roswell belonged to us?"

"I'm afraid so, Mr Rossi."

The group, apart from Gorman, couldn't believe what they were hearing. The most legendary incident of all UFO stories was a craft built by the United States.

"Well, I'll be dammed," said Curtis. "All these years."

"But if our government gave you orders to try and copy the alien craft, why didn't work continue?" asked Hoffman.

"Because after the disaster a government official at the White House ordered us to abandon the idea of trying to replicate the spacecraft and proceed with designing more conventional weapons. But if they'd have given us more time, Mr Hoffman," said Saltzman clenching his fist in anger. "If they'd only given us more time, who knows, we could have made it work."

"So why didn't you tell the media that the craft that crashed at Roswell belonged to us?" asked Rossi.

"There's a very simple explanation for that," said Gorman.

"Since that incident, we've been able to use the UFO phenomenon to our advantage. It means that we can build and test-fly all types of experimental military aircraft without being concerned whether the American public or the Russians see them."

"You mean by allowing the people and our enemies to believe they've seen a UFO and that acts as a cover for our military test fights?" asked Hoffman.

"Correct," said Gorman.

There was silence for a moment before Hoffman continued.

"So let me get this straight. You have in your possession an extraterrestrial spacecraft which was discovered by you, Colonel, in January 1947. That spacecraft was then delivered here, and then copied with disastrous consequences. You were then told by the government not to proceed in trying to duplicate this machine, which you've obviously ignored."

"Oh no, we didn't ignore it," interrupted Saltzman. "We stopped building flying disk aircraft because of the accidents and loss of test pilots, but we continued to copy the technology from the spacecraft that we were capable of using."

"And now you feel this object on the moon could be another spaceship. Is that right?"

"That's right, and that's why we're not prepared to tell Kennedy," said Gorman. "If he knew about this he'd want to bring the space programme forward, putting more pressure on people, and causing more accidents."

"Well I don't agree," replied Hoffman. "I'm sure that if I spoke to Kennedy and told him what we have here, he'd see things your way."

"Well, it's a chance were not willing to take," said Saltzman.

Curtis began to understand the concern that Saltzman and Gorman had. In his career as an air force pilot and C.I.A agent, he had seen the consequences of too much government interference which had led to so many men getting killed.

"Come on chief," he said quietly. "They have a point. Let's find out what we're dealing with, and then we can decide what action to take."

Saltzman walked towards Hoffman. He placed his hand on the C.I.A chief's shoulder.

"Mr Hoffman, I understand your feelings, but will you try to understand our position?

We've been in possession of this alien spacecraft for the last sixteen years. Where do these people come from, Mr Hoffman? Why did they come here and more importantly, what do they want? These are the questions that the Professor and I have been asking all this time. Its people like us that need to find these answers, not politicians."

"There's something else you should know," continued Gorman.

"Do you know that Kennedy's been trying to do a deal with Khrushchev? He wants Russia and the United States to work together to put a U.S astronaut and Russian Cosmonaut on the moon together. Do you know about that?"

Hoffman looked at Curtis for a moment then said reluctantly, "Yes I know about it, and I have to say it's not a popular deal he's trying to make."

Curtis was surprised at what he was hearing. This was the first time he'd heard anything about this. "What's this all about chief, what deal?"

"Kennedy's been trying to achieve better relations with the Russians. He feels that if the two countries were able to work together on this, it may bring about better relations between us. Maybe an end to the cold war, and perhaps more cooperation."

"And what do you think?"

Hoffman shrugged his shoulders. "He's got good intentions, but would it work?"

"The answer to that, Mr Hoffman, is no," said Gorman. "He's trying to do a deal with a man who, just over a year ago, tried to place nuclear missiles ninety miles off our coast. Would you do a deal with him? And as for letting that commie bastard know about our project, he can go to hell."

"So you see, Mr Hoffman," said Saltzman. "There are reasons for keeping all of this from Kennedy. We must keep this to ourselves until we know more about this object and its origin."

Curtis and Hoffman looked at each other. Both of them knew the Americans had to reach the moon first to investigate whatever it was that was on the lunar surface. If Saltzman's aerospace company were the people to achieve it, then it would be in the best interest if the C.I.A were involved. At least they'd know what was happening. Hoffman walked across to the central sofa and sat down. He picked up the photographs and looked hard at them, wondering if he should tell John Kennedy, or whether or not he should work alongside Saltzman and Majestic. Finally he made his decision.

"Okay Saltzman, what do you want to do?"

The industrialist smiled as he felt the head of the C.I.A was now about to commit the agency in what would be the first ever private expedition to the moon.

"First of all gentlemen, I want to launch our new improved lunar orbiter that will send back images far superior to the ones we already have."

"How do you plan to do this?" asked Rossi.

"With a camera fitted with lenses that have better magnification than the ones we used on our last mission. It's important we get a closer look at the object, so our spacecraft will be placed in a lower orbit."

"How low are we going?" asked Gorman.

"Thirty nautical miles."

"What about N.A.S.A, are they planning any lunar surveillance?" asked Curtis.

"No, not yet. They're too busy preparing the two man Gemini program. They won't be planning any surveillance for another three years, and that, gentlemen, is far too long for us to wait."

Hoffman, still studying the photographs, said, "I should imagine the Russians are still sending probes to study this?"

"Oh, I should imagine they are, and that's why I need the C.I.A. It will be your job to keep an eye on the Soviets at all times. If they send up a fire cracker we need to know."

Hoffman began to see the consequences of a three-year delay. He felt the CIA had to assist Saltzman Aerospace and Majestic in achieving their goal.

"When can you get this orbiter of yours ready?" asked Gorman.

"As you know gentlemen, I own eight major aerospace complexes around the United States. I also have a number of subsidiary companies around the world. All of them are making various components for our lunar orbiter. None of them know anything about our mission of course. When the components arrive here, the jigsaw is put together by my people."

"Do the technicians here know what the orbiter is going to photograph?" asked Hoffman.

"No. They know we're going to photograph the moon surface, but we'll tell them we're looking for landing sites for the Apollo program."

"So when are you planning to launch the orbiter?" asked Rossi.

"November 19th. It will be launched from this base using an Atlas-Agena D rocket."

Saltzman crossed the room to his desk. "Gentlemen, would you gather round please?"

As the five men approached the desk, Professor Steiner broke from the group and walked to a large painting of a world war two B25 flying fortress hanging on the wall.

"Now, if you'd like to keep your eyes on the painting," said the professor.

Saltzman pressed a button on the side of his desk. Instantly the painting revolved one hundred and eighty degrees on a central pivot, revealing a blueprint of the lunar orbiter.

"There you have it gentlemen, our latest lunar probe. Professor Steiner, would you like to explain?"

Steiner walked to the blueprint and began to point out various sections of the spacecraft.

"Well, the vehicle is really an orbiting photographic laboratory.

If you look at the lower section of the spacecraft you'll notice we have a six hundred and ten millimetre, narrow angle, high resolution lens. It has a fixed aperture of five point six to allow as much light through the lens as possible. An aperture any wider would result in depth of field problems, ruining the final image."

"How long does the shutter stay open?" asked Rossi.

"Approximately eight seconds."

Steiner pointed out a series of gears and pulleys on the blueprint. "Because the shutter stays open so long, we have to prevent motion blurring of the image. We have achieved this by attaching the film to these gear wheels. A tiny electric motor turns these wheels and pulls the film through a series of pinch rollers. The mechanism has been carefully calculated to compensate for the velocity of the spacecraft."

"How's the film developed?" asked Gorman.

Steiner pointed at the processing unit, which was a box about twelve inches square.

"The film is finally pulled into this small processing tank. The film is already coated with conventional dark room chemicals and heat inside the tank processes the film. Light is then flashed through the resulting negative creating beams that are converted into electrical signals. It's these signals which are transmitted back to earth where a final black-and-white image is created."

"So if our launching is on the nineteenth, when do you expect to see the first set of photographs?" asked Hoffman.

"We hope to have the first set of images ready within eight hours of transmission from the moon," replied Saltzman.

Hoffman looked at the prints once more. "Okay, so what if this object turns out to be another alien spacecraft, you can't reach it until we know how to land on the moon. Now that's not going to be until the end of this decade, so what are we supposed to do till then?"

"Absolutely nothing," smiled Saltzman. We let N.A.S.A do all the work and once their Apollo moon programme is cut short we'll launch our mission."

"What do you mean, cut short?" asked Curtis. "How are you going to do that?"

"By cutting the funding," said Gorman. "Once we've been to the moon three or four times, we'll have proven to the Russians that we are technically superior."

"But what about our mission?" asked Rossi. "What explanation do we give for that trip?"

"We tell them that it's a scientific mission," said Saltzman.

"All of the N.A.S.A personnel will be replaced by Saltzman aerospace technicians at Cape Canaveral, and I will take control of the operation."

Curtis who had been listening carefully to all this, felt there could be a problem.

"I think you're overlooking something, Saltzman. In a couple of years' time, N.A.S.A is going to be sending its own probes to photograph the moon. What happens if they stumble across this object?"

"I'm afraid that's something we'll have to deal with if it happens, Mr Curtis."

"Do remember, Steve, N.A.S.A know nothing about all of this," said Rossi. "When they start photographing the moon, they'll be looking for landing sites for the lunar module, they won't be looking for anything else."

There was silence in the room for a moment. Saltzman walked across to Hoffman and shook his hand.

"Thank you, James. I hope you see how important it is for our country to reach the moon first. If there is something on the lunar surface, I want it to be in our hands, not the Russians."

"Well, I agree with you on that, but I still think Kennedy should know. He's a great man."

Saltzman shook his head. "No, please let's keep him out of this. We'll tell him when the time's right."

Gorman stood up and spoke to the group. "Gentlemen, can I suggest we meet at the end of November, say the twenty eighth, by then we'll have some results from our spacecraft."

Saltzman looked at Hoffman seeking his approval.

"Agreed," said the CIA chief. "The twenty eighth it is. Steve let's go."

The two C.I.A men turned away from the group and headed towards the lift leaving Saltzman, Gorman, Rossi, and the professor behind.

"Well, I think it's time for another drink Vigo, don't you?" said Gorman quietly.

"Absolutely," said the industrialist. "Professor Steiner, Lieutenant, would you join us?"

The four men gathered around the cocktail bar as Hoffman and Curtis made their ascent to the surface level.

"Well chief, what do you make of what we've seen and heard today?"

"I can understand the need for secrecy," said Hoffman. "But it's my opinion this is too big for just a small number of people to monopolise. Remember when N.A.S.A was set up by President Eisenhower. It was his wish that it would be outside of military control. Now something's been discovered, the military want to run the show, and I think that's dangerous."

Just then the lift came to a gentle halt. Slowly the doors opened and the two men walked briskly to the security desk. Unclipping their I.D badges they handed them back to the secretary who had just finished typing out the daily reports.

"Thank you gentlemen, I trust you've had an interesting day?"

"Yes we have," replied Hoffman. "Very interesting."

Both men turned and walked to the exit door. It was early evening and the heat of the sun had now diminished leaving the desert air warm and dry.

"So what are you planning?" asked Curtis, as they stood waiting for their transport. "Are you going to tell Kennedy?"

"You bet your life I'm going to tell him. I also think it's time someone looked into the operations of Majestic. I'm sure they must know a lot more than they're telling us." Hoffman looked at Curtis. "How on earth is a country supposed to function when we've got so many groups operating under their own rules and talking to no-one else? I think you and I had better start searching for some answers too."

Down in the underground headquarters, Rossi, Gorman, Professor Steiner, and Saltzman were still talking amongst themselves.

"Well lieutenant Rossi, do you like the idea of being the commander of our Apollo mission?" asked Saltzman.

"I like the idea very much."

"You must understand that it means you won't be the first man to walk on the moon, does this sadden you?"

"Mr Saltzman, when I think we could be discovering something more important than just recovering moon rock, it doesn't worry me in the slightest."

"Good man, good man," replied Saltzman, patting the young pilot on the shoulder.

Saltzman then walked across to Gorman who was talking quietly to the professor.

"Colonel, can I have a word with you?"

There was a sound of concern in Saltzman's voice as if he feared something was going wrong. He gently maneuverered Gorman away from the other men so he could talk to him privately.

"Colonel, it's been brought to my attention that the president has been made aware of what we have here. Do you know anything about it?"

"In what way has he been notified?" replied Gorman calmly.

"Apparently he's been receiving letters from some anonymous source." Saltzman turned and looked Gorman in the eye. "I do hope that all the members of your group know where there allegiances lie Colonel."

Gorman wasn't pleased with what Saltzman was suggesting. "What do you mean?"

Saltzman slowly shrugged his shoulders. "Well it wasn't anyone at this base, the security's too tight. Have you any ideas who it could be?"

"Not at this time, but I'll find out Vigo, I'll find out. As for Kennedy, plans have already been made to make sure he never asks us any questions." Gorman raised his whiskey glass.

"Cheers Vigo."

chapter three
QUESTIONS

November 22nd, 1963: 1.30pm

Steve Curtis stood gazing out of an office window at Hahn airbase, West Germany. The installation had been taken over by the United States in 1952, making it the seventh largest U.S airbase in Europe. Located high on a ridge, one thousand six hundred and fifty feet above sea level, the base was well situated for the Americans. If the Soviet Union decided to launch an attack, the U.S were capable of reaching all locations in Europe and the Mediterranean regions in a short time. Curtis had been sent to the base by his C.I.A chief James Hoffman. The purpose was to question Colonel Peter Davis who, in January 1947 along with John Gorman, retrieved an alien spacecraft from the New Mexico desert. Both Hoffman and Curtis felt there was more to the UFO story than what Gorman had told them four weeks earlier at Area 51. By hearing Davis's account, the C.I.A hoped to learn more about the incident. Curtis gazed across the airfield. It was a damp misty afternoon in the German mountains, but the winter conditions didn't stop the Cold War operations of the military. An air force pilot at the controls of an F-86 Sabre fighter had taxied his aircraft to the end of the main runway. The fighter stood motionless for a few moments before the pilot opened the throttle. A deafening roar came from the aircraft as it began to accelerate, its after-burner hurling tail-fire like a giant blow torch from the rear of the fuselage. The nose of the aircraft began to lift and, with the grace of an eagle, the war machine rose into the air, its undercarriage quickly retracting. The roaring sound of the engine began to fade as it disappeared into the mist, and the only sound that remained was the noise of a military vehicle on the east side of the airbase.

The door of the office opened. Curtis turned and saw the six foot two inch air force Colonel standing in the doorway. Davis was forty eight years old now, but still remained the slim fit military man he had been his entire career.

"Mr Curtis?"

"Yes. Good afternoon Colonel. Thank you for taking the time to see me," said Curtis as he crossed the room to shake Davis's hand.

"Please sit down. It isn't often I have to deal directly with the C.I.A, so I know this must be important."

Both men walked across to the desk in the left corner of the room. There were two identical black leather swivel chairs either side of the desk. Curtis sat down on one of them and placed an A4 size writing pad on his knee.

"It seems you're planning to ask a lot of questions. May I ask what this is all about?" smiled Davis as he sat down and faced Curtis.

Curtis looked at the Colonel wondering how he would react once he began to ask him about the UFO incident in 1947. After all it had been a long time ago and Davis, like all the other men that recovered the alien spacecraft, had been told to keep quiet.

"Okay Colonel, I'll come straight to the point. I want to talk to you about the crashed spacecraft you and a number of other men discovered sixteen years ago."

There was a moment's silence as both men stared at each other. The smile on Davis's face was quickly replaced with a look of shock.

"Do you mind if I get a drink?"

"No not at all."

He got up and crossed to the filing cabinet five feet away from him. Opening the top drawer he removed a bottle of Scotch and two whisky glasses.

"It's okay, I don't normally drink when I'm on duty, but in this case I'll make an exception. Would you like one?"

"No thanks."

Davis poured himself a whisky then sat down to face Curtis. "I was given orders never to talk about that spacecraft, Mr Curtis. After sixteen years, why the sudden interest?"

Curtis knew he wouldn't be able to tell Davis everything, but in order to find out more he would have to trust Davis with some information.

"Well, I'm sure you appreciate security in this matter Colonel.

You'll just have to trust me on this and accept I can't tell you too much. But I'd be grateful if you could give me your account of the event."

Davis took a deep breath and thought for a moment before he began to speak.

"Well, the object was picked up on our radar late in the evening.

I remember taking a look at the scope and noticing the phenomenal speed of the craft. I realized it wasn't ours and we were almost certain that it didn't belong to the Russians."

As Davis spoke, Curtis took a pen from the inside of his jacket and began to write down Davis's version of that night.

"Colonel, did you believe at any time the vehicle on your radar scope was extraterrestrial?"

"Yes I did. I'd always believed that it was possible that these things existed after talking to many of our airmen. Many of them were convinced that they'd seen unidentified objects while flying missions. So in a way I was hoping it would be alien."

"Okay so you set off and located the spacecraft. What happened after that?" asked Curtis.

He was eager to press on with the story. He was interested to hear how Davis's account of that night compared with Gorman's version.

"Well, Colonel Gorman told me to stay with the rest of the men while he investigated the spacecraft. We all watched him climb inside, then after about ten minutes he reappeared. I was anxious to know what he'd found. I'd never seen anything like this before, and wanted to know about the crew. What were they like? Where were they from? And more importantly, were they alive? But sadly, the pilot was dead."

"What happened then?"

"Well, we took the craft back to our base, and then next day Gorman told us that everything had to be packed up and taken to Wright airbase. I never saw or heard anything of it again."

Curtis continued to write down the Davis's account. So far his story was the same as Gorman's.

"Colonel, just one more question. Do you know what happened to the alien?"

"Which one?"

Curtis stopped writing. He looked up from his notepad and glared at Davis.

"What do you mean which one?"

"Which alien are you talking about? There were two of them. There was the dead alien inside the craft and the injured one which they found the next day."

Curtis couldn't believe what he was hearing. He suspected there could be another alien, but he didn't expect this from Davis. He sat up in his chair and leaned forward. "So there was a live alien?"

"Sure. It was found by Colonel Roy Kramer and helicopter pilot Richard Maguire."

"Colonel Kramer, who's he?"

"He was in charge of security and counter intelligence. Once the craft was reported by Gorman, Colonel Kramer took over. They found the alien three miles from the crash site."

Davis began to tell Curtis the story.

January 11th, 1947: The Day After The Alien Craft Was Found

A U.S air force helicopter flew low over the New Mexico landscape, the morning after the alien craft was discovered. The two men inside had been airborne since midday. General Glenn had ordered Kramer to take a look at the crash site and the surrounding area just in case something had been missed by Gorman and his team.

It was late afternoon, but Colonel Kramer wanted to check a wider area of the site personally. From the starboard side of the craft, Kramer glanced down at the rocky terrain below. The frustration of finding nothing after flying for such a long time was beginning to show on him as he became more irritable. Suddenly pilot Maguire called out, "Colonel, look, sir, over there at the base of those rocks."

Kramer leaned forward and looked out of the port side of the craft. At first he saw nothing but the dry dusty ground littered with rocks. Then, glistening in the bright sunlight, a small round silver object attracted his attention. Raising his binoculars to take a closer look, he noticed the object gently moving around like a silver balloon in the desert breeze.

"Take her down, I think we've found something," said Kramer.

Maguire began to reduce the throttle with the left hand lever, while controlling the pitch and roll of the aircraft with the joystick mounted in front of him. As the helicopter began a slow descent into a clear area,

Kramer continued to keep his eyes on the silver object. Maguire gently brought the aircraft closer to the target. As the machine made a soft landing in the desert dust, Kramer climbed out and ran to what appeared to be a weather balloon. It was six feet in diameter and made of a leather material. It was warm and smooth and Kramer could press his hand a good two inches into it. Maguire came and stood next to the Colonel.

"Any idea what it is, sir?"

"It seems hollow that's for sure," replied Kramer as he began to walk slowly around the sphere, gently pressing the surface with both hands. Then a tiny section felt hard as if a metal plate was fixed to the inside of the strange object. He pressed firmly against the thick silver skin attempting to place his fingers around the back of the plate. Suddenly a loud hiss, like the sound of escaping air, came from the top of the sphere.

The whole object began to deflate, splitting down the centre as escaping gas rushed out. Kramer and Maguire quickly grasped one side of the torn sections and began to pull the sphere apart with their bare hands. Then both of them stopped, staring at the contents inside.

A tiny man, about four feet in height, lay motionless inside.

The men crouched down either side of the alien, and then Maguire slowly rolled the corpse into Kramer's arms.

They looked down at the young face of the humanoid alien. His skin was very smooth and had a light brown tan. He had a thick crop of blond hair which was combed forward with a fringe cut halfway down his forehead. Maguire lay the alien's tiny left-hand across the palm of his own and gazed at the man's long thin fingers. Unknown to the young helicopter pilot and Kramer, the alien was an exact replica of the one found by Colonel Gorman the night before.

Suddenly the alien took a deep breath and began gasping for air.

"Jesus Christ, he's alive," shouted Kramer.

The alien gripped Maguire's hand as he continued to gasp and cough.

He opened his beautiful blue eyes and stared at the pilot as if in a desperate plea for help.

"Colonel, there's a small oxygen cylinder and mask behind the pilot's seat, fetch it, sir, quickly."

Kramer rose to his feet and ran to the helicopter while Maguire fought desperately to assist the alien's breathing.

"Don't die my friend, please don't die," said the pilot in desperation, as he cradled the tiny man in his arms trying to give him some reassurance. Kramer returned with the breathing apparatus and quickly placed the mask over the alien's mouth.

"Try to breathe slowly," said Maguire trying hard to communicate. The man nodded his head. He began to breathe normally as if he could understand what was being said.

"Let's get him out of here before anyone else arrives on the scene," said Kramer. "The fewer people know about him the better."

"But where do we take him, sir?"

Kramer looked around him. The New Mexico desert was all around them. "How much fuel do we have?"

"We can reach base easily enough, but we have enough fuel for at least ninety miles."

"That's far enough," thought Kramer. The Colonel knew that the best place to take the alien was a top security base away from the eyes of the media.

"Okay, let's get him on board the chopper, and I'll tell you where I want you to take us."

"Sir, what about the remains of the sphere, won't someone find it?"

"Okay, you get him on board and I'll collect this up."

Maguire gently picked up the alien and ran to the helicopter Kramer began to roll up the deflated sphere, and then followed the pilot back to the aircraft.

Within minutes they were airborne and heading north to a destination known only to Kramer.

As Davis finished his story, Curtis sat quietly thinking.

"Why weren't we told about the second alien?" he thought to himself. "Why have Saltzman and Gorman kept it quiet? Maybe even they weren't aware that another alien had been found."

"Everything all right, Mr Curtis?" asked Davis.

"Yes, I'm fine. Did you ever find out where the second alien was taken?"

"Yes. It was a secret military hospital they reserved for foreign spies who had been injured during arrest."

"How did you come to know the rest of the story?"

"About the second alien you mean? I was stationed here with Maguire three months after the episode. One day we sat together and he told me what happened. He'd been told to keep quiet like the rest of us, but he felt he needed to talk to someone about it. Of course when he chose to tell me I knew exactly what incident he was talking about."

"Did you tell him your side of the story?"

"No. I've kept quiet. What happened that night has never troubled me enough to have to tell someone. I've always wanted to know more of course, but I've always put it to the back of my mind."

"Is Maguire still around?"

"I'm afraid not, he was killed in a training mission two years ago."

"Damn," said Curtis. He was hoping that the pilot could give more information about the second alien. "Did Maguire tell you what they did with the alien once they reached the security base?"

"Yes. He said they took him from the helicopter, placed him in an ambulance and rushed him to surgery.

That was the last time he ever saw the alien or Kramer again. He was told to leave the base immediately, keep his mouth shut and never return or he could find himself in trouble."

"I take it Kramer stayed at the base?"

"Apparently."

Curtis couldn't understand why Kramer had been allowed to stay at the base. Was it because of his rank? He couldn't be sure, but it was something he felt he would have to look more deeply into.

"Well, I'd like to thank you for talking to me Colonel; you've cleared up a couple of things that were troubling us."

"Oh my pleasure, I wish you could tell me more, but I understand the need for secrecy. I take it you're staying till tomorrow morning?"

"That's right. I hope you don't mind."

"Not at all," smiled Davis.

Curtis stood up and shook the Colonel's hand. He was grateful for Davis's co-operation and hospitality and he had learned a lot more.

"I have to write out some reports so I'll do my best to keep out of your way."

"That's no problem. If you'd like to follow me I'll show you to your room."

The two men walked across the room to the door.

"Would you like to join me and some of the other officers for a drink tonight? You'll find some of them have got their own UFO stories to tell."

"That'll be interesting," said Curtis.

"Right, I'll send someone to collect you from your room at eight thirty."

"Eight thirty? That'll be fine."

That evening Curtis finished writing out his reports which he would present to James Hoffman at the C.I.A headquarters. Suddenly there was a loud knock on the door. He looked at his watch. "They're early," he thought. He quickly packed his report and reference notes into his case and snapped it shut. Briskly he walked across the room and opened the door expecting an air force Lieutenant to be standing there. It was Davis, and he looked shocked.

"Colonel?" said Curtis noticing the concern on the man's face.

"Steve, President Kennedy's been shot."

Both men stood motionless with shock for a moment before Curtis spoke.

"How is he?"

"I'm not sure, but it looks bad."

"How, for God's sake?" asked Curtis angrily. "We were supposed to have our people watching his every move. I can't believe it. What the hell happened?"

"He was in an open-top limousine. The motorcade was travelling through the streets in Dallas on its way to the trade mart when the shots rang out."

"Open-top limousine?" Curtis was furious. "He should have never been put in a situation like that. Are the reports still coming through?"

"Yes, in my office."

Quickly closing the door behind him, Curtis charged down the corridor with Davis following. What chaos could the United States be thrown into now, wondered Curtis. Several scenarios raced through his mind. Would Lyndon Johnson take over as President if Kennedy died? If so, would Kennedy's plans to withdraw troops from Vietnam be destroyed, leaving thousands of American troops to die? Would the Russians take advantage of the situation and try once again to equip Cuba with ballistic missiles? The situation was frightening but there was nothing Curtis could do at this moment but pray.

As they reached Davis's office there were already three senior Air force personnel listening to the broadcast. Like Curtis they were shocked, at the events in Dallas. One of the officers, almost in tears, turned to the two men and said in a solemn voice, "Kennedy's dead."

Curtis slowly walked to a chair and slumped into it as if all the strength from his body had been drained from him.

"I've got to get back to America," he said quietly. "I've got to get back right away."

"I'll get a plane ready," said Davis.

The assassination of President John Fitzgerald Kennedy soon spread and people from all corners of the world stood united in grief. It was as if the light of a better future for all mankind had been taken away. As the shocked world watched and listened to the episode of events in Texas, a team of thirty five men headed by Vigo Saltzman and Professor Gerhard Steiner sat glued to their computer screens at Area 51. Their tiny lunar orbiter had spent the last three days hurtling through the void of space and was now only minutes away from entering orbit around the moon.

"Two minutes to orbital capture," announced the guidance technician.

"Splendid," replied Saltzman.

He sat at the back of the thirty foot square control room with Professor Steiner. In front of them sat four rows of computers, seven in each row and all of them were manned.

Each of the technicians sat scrutinizing the data sent back from the lunar orbiter.

"Well Professor, it won't be long now," he said quietly. "If all goes to plan we should be receiving the best quality photographs of that alien craft yet seen."

"Well, you'll have to wait for the processing to be completed before you see your results Vigo, can you wait that long?" smiled Steiner.

None of the technical team dared to look away from their monitors. Every piece of data was being analysed and decoded ready for the next phase.

"Five seconds," shouted the guidance technician. "Four, three, two, one."

A quarter of a million miles away, the three hundred and eight kilogram spacecraft swung into lunar orbit, disappearing round the far side of the moon. The guidance technician swivelled round in his chair to face Saltzman and Steiner.

"We have it confirmed, sir. Our spacecraft is now in a thirty mile orbit above the lunar surface."

"Excellent," said Saltzman.

The industrialist made his way from the rear of the control room, patting the backs of some of the technicians as he walked past them. He turned and faced his team.

"Gentlemen, I congratulate you all. Our spacecraft is now in orbit and will soon be photographing the Sinus Medii region of the moon. We should be receiving the results within a few hours, and hopefully we will learn more about this area of the lunar surface."

As Saltzman and his team continued to celebrate, an American air force transport plane flew high over the Atlantic. Steve Curtis was heading back to the U.S, his mind asking hundreds of questions. Why had President Kennedy been assassinated?

Who was responsible and what was the reason? Why had he been allowed to sit in the back of an open top car, making him a clear target for any assassin? As the questions raced through his mind, the co-pilot emerged from the cockpit.

"Mr Curtis?"

"Yes?"

"We've been ordered to divert to Florida and take you to Cape Canaveral."

"Why, for God's sake?" asked the confused agent.

Curtis couldn't understand why he wasn't being flown back to C.I.A headquarters at Langley. The whole world was in shock over the assassination of President Kennedy, yet he was being diverted to Florida.

"Has any reason been given?" he asked.

"No, sir. We were just told to get you to Cape Canaveral right away."

Curtis paused for a moment. "Why for God's sake?" he thought. "Okay thanks."

He was completely confused by the entire situation. He sat back in his seat and gazed out the window. As he looked out, he watched the starboard wing tilt gently downwards as the aircraft began to bank on its new heading. He knew there was nothing he could do until he reached Florida, where he hoped some answers would finally be found.

At area 51 the mood was totally different. An excited team of technicians, Vigo Saltzman and Professor Steiner, were waiting for their tiny space probe to burst into life. The lunar orbiter had now emerged from the dark side of the moon, and its signals were being received clearly by the control team.

"Orbit correct, sir," said the mission controller.

"Well Gerhard, here we go," said Saltzman rubbing his hands with excitement at the prospect of having high resolution close up images of what he hoped would be another alien spacecraft.

The technicians began to concentrate on the signals being sent back to them, as they kept a close vigil on the orbiter. A quarter of a million miles away and thirty miles above the lunar surface, the orbiter's electronic systems had begun to operate. The eighty millimetre telephoto lens on board the spacecraft was now bearing down on its target. As it approached the area the shutter on the lens opened. Immediately a tiny electric motor began to wind the film through its sprocket wheels in perfect synchronization to match the velocity of the spacecraft. Gradually, frame by frame, image by image, the orbiter photographed the entire area. The barren lifeless landscape appeared to resemble Plaster-of-Paris in colour and texture. Its grey, powdery looking surface had been bombarded for centuries by meteors, some the size of large boulders, others as tiny particles.

This high velocity meteoric rain had fallen when the moon was still very young. As the surface was punctured, basalt had oozed to the surface while the young world still obtained its molten core.

Rocks from deep within the moon had been blasted to the surface by some of the larger impacts, while the lunar mountains had soft rounded edges to them. The orbiter functioned perfectly as it flew over the crater Ukert. Then, seventy five miles to the west, a shiny object on the lunar surface came into view. The camera shutter opened, recording a perfect image. Then another frame of film was exposed. One after another in two minute intervals the tiny craft shot the pictures Saltzman was so keen to set his hands on. All that remained now was for the on board processing unit to develop the film and transmit the image back to earth.

November 22nd, 1963: Midnight Eastern Standard Time

Steve Curtis walked down the small ladder of the transport plane which had landed at Cape Canaveral. Standing twelve feet away from the aircraft, next to a small army vehicle, was a military security officer.

"Mr Curtis?" said the six foot New Yorker. "I'm Sergeant Harrison Price. I've been sent to meet and brief you on the situation. Would you like to climb into the back of this jeep please?"

Curtis climbed into the rear of the vehicle followed by Price. "Okay, take us to the security block."

Without questioning the order the driver switched on the engine. "First of all, Mr Curtis, I've been asked to give you this."

Price handed Curtis a sealed brown A4 envelope. From the feel of it, there wasn't much information inside for Curtis to read.

"What's this?" he asked.

"I don't know, sir. I was asked to pass it on to you by James Hoffman."

"I wonder if it as something to do with Kennedy's assassination," he thought to himself.

"I don't know what's in the envelope, sir, but I do know why you're here. You've been asked by Mr Hoffman to interrogate a man who tried to destroy one of our rockets."

"What? When the hell did this happen?" said Curtis in disbelief. He found it unbelievable that N.A.S.A could be so careless about with their security.

"Today, of all days. Apparently he is obsessed with stopping us from reaching the moon and exploring space itself. Apparently he'd been writing to the President for months telling him that we shouldn't even make an attempt at space travel, because of the terrible dangers it could bring on all of us. He even claims he knows about a government cover up on a major UFO incident."

Curtis now knew why Hoffman had diverted him to the Cape. Had this man information that could help the C.I.A, and how much did he really know about UFO's?

The car arrived at one of the security buildings. As it stopped Curtis noticed two military police standing outside the door.

"Whoever the man is, he's heavily guarded," remarked Curtis as he climbed out of the car.

Price led the C.I.A agent past the two guards. Inside the office block another guard stood outside a door leading to a small room.

"Okay, do you want to talk to him alone?" asked Price.

"Sure," replied Curtis bracing himself for the encounter with this man.

The security officer opened the door and Curtis walked in, closing it behind him. He stood still for a moment and gazed around the room. The man he was about to interrogate sat with his back to Curtis, and made no attempt to turn and face him. The only furniture in the room was a wooden chair that the man sat on, a small table in front of him and another chair opposite. Curtis slowly approached the table. He pulled his chair towards him and sat down to face the man. It was then he was taken totally by surprise. Facing Curtis was a priest, in his early forties, slim, and about five feet ten in height. He was clean-shaven and his brown hair was combed neatly.

"Sir?" said the priest.

Curtis looked at him for a moment. "They tell me you've caused some damage to an N.A.S.A rocket, is that right?"

Without hesitating the man answered in a firm, confident voice. "That's right, I have," he said as he sat back in his chair, hands clasped and looking straight at Curtis without any sign of fear of his interrogator.

Curtis stared back for a moment before he continued. "Look, my name's Steve Curtis, what's yours?"

"Reverend Kidman, Paul Kidman."

Curtis stopped and thought for a moment. He'd heard that name before, but where?

"Okay Reverend, as you know, President Kennedy's wish was that the United States of America should commit itself to land a man on the moon. Do you have a problem with this?"

Kidman leaned forward in his chair. "I most certainly do, Mr Curtis."

"May I ask why?" asked Curtis calmly.

"Because Kennedy is.... or should I say, was, making a terrible mistake."

"Mistake? About what? Wanting to further man's knowledge about the universe?"

"You really believe that? That it was to further man's knowledge?"

Kidman paused for a moment as he glared at Curtis.

"Have you ever considered what we might find out there… out there in space, Mr Curtis? Do you think we could handle anything we found?"

"I don't understand what you mean, handle anything we found?"

Kidman then stood up and began to walk slowly towards the edge of the room. He turned around and casually put his hands in his pockets, then leaned against the wall and said, "Do you think mankind has developed enough to cope with an intelligence years more advanced than himself, Mr Curtis?"

Curtis thought for a moment. He knew Saltzman and his industry were trying to copy the alien technology. Some of it had been successful, while there had been failures in other areas.

He knew he must not give anything away, although he had to try and answer the priest.

"Well, I think if we came across such intelligence, we'd have to try and understand it," said Curtis.

"What if that intelligence fell into the wrong hands?" continued Kidman. The priest paused for a moment, never taking his eyes off Curtis. "You know the real reason for this race to the moon, don't you?"

"Go on," said Curtis, hoping to find out the real motive for Kidman's actions.

"Well it's got nothing to do with space exploration that's for sure," said Kidman as he began to walk back to his chair. He sat down, looked straight at Curtis and said, "It's all about beating the Russians. Plain and simple. Egos, Mr Curtis, that's all it is. While nations starve to death we and the Russians spend millions on rockets to the moon. Have you thought about the price of this adventure, that's if we do make it to the moon?"

"I can think of the terrible price if we don't," replied Curtis.

"Oh, so you support all of this… this flying to the moon?" asked Kidman

"Yes I do, and as sure as hell we'll make it and we'll return having learnt more about ourselves."

"Mr Curtis, you know as well as I do that space travel is just another way to show technical supremacy over the rest of the world. Flexing our muscle and improving on more destructive ways to destroy each other. Do you know that we have the power to destroy ourselves ten times over?"

"Yes I know that, but I don't think we will. Mankind isn't that stupid. There's too much to lose. We know that and so do the Russians."

"Yes, but all it takes is one mad man, that's all, just one.

That man does not have to be Russian or American. He could be a terrorist from any part of the world. Don't you see that, Mr Curtis?"

"Yes, I understand what you're saying, but such men can and will be stopped, now and in the future. We can't let such people stop man from progressing."

There was a moment's pause as both men thought about what the other had said.

"I wish I shared the same faith in mankind as you, Mr Curtis," said Kidman quietly.

Curtis looked at Kidman for a moment then said, "Look, I wouldn't say that I'm a great religious man, but I wouldn't call myself an atheist either. Surely Jesus had faith in mankind. Why do you think he'd come to this earth and tell us to love and care for each other if he knew we weren't capable of doing so? Surely he wouldn't have given his life to a lost cause."

There was another moment of silence before Kidman spoke.

"Yes I… I understand, but then there's all this sending men into space. Who knows what or who we might find out there? Races of people more advanced than us and of course more dangerous."

"Yes, but who's to say they would be more dangerous than us. I'd like to think one day mankind will have learnt to be at peace with its self."

There was a moment of piece in the room between both men before Curtis continued.

"Before the president was killed I understand you wrote to Mr Kennedy about some government cover-up concerning a UFO incident. Now is that true?"

"I don't wish to talk about that, sir," said Kidman gazing across the room.

Curtis knew he had to make the priest talk, so he tried to provoke Kidman.

"Okay then, I'll take it that wasn't true. Personally I think these stories about spacemen and flying saucers are made up by crack pot people talking utter nonsense."

"Nonsense you say? I can assure you these things exist," said the priest in a frightened voice.

"How do you know?"

"Because I've seen them," said Kidman leaning forward across the table. "When I was stationed at the White Sands missile base in 1947 we recovered a spacecraft from the desert, Mr Curtis."

Suddenly the agent knew the man he was talking too. "That's were I've heard his name," he thought to himself. "He was one of Gorman's team."

Curtis was aware that he couldn't tell the priest that he knew about the alien craft, but felt this was a good opportunity to try and learn a little more.

"Well, what happened to this spacecraft?"

"When we brought it back to our base at White Sands it was placed in a hangar with the rest of the debris we'd been told to collect. Then our Colonel told us that everything had to be packed up and moved out. An engineer by the name of Gene Kane and I placed the final case on board the transport plane. We were so curious about this case we just had to take a look inside. So we made sure there was no one around then we opened it."

"What did you see?" asked Curtis.

"A tiny man lay inside. He was dead of course, but what a beautiful man. Not a blemish on his skin, his blonde hair just shone, Mr Curtis, and he had eyes which were as blue as the sky itself. He looked so perfect I just wish you could have seen him."

Curtis sat quietly for a moment before continuing. "Did anything happen after that?"

"I never saw or heard of the spaceship or the alien again. We were told to keep quiet and say nothing to anyone, but Gene couldn't resist. Once they found out he'd been talking to a young journalist called Hannon, he was arrested and questioned for days. They made his life hell, Mr Curtis."

"Who made his life hell?" pressed the agent. He wanted to know who was responsible.

Kidman raised his arms in desperation. "We just don't know. We couldn't find out. What I do know, Mr Curtis, is that anyone who talks about that incident or tries to find answers disappears or gets killed."

"And is that what happened to Kane?"

Kidman nodded. "He was found hanging in his cell two weeks after being arrested."

"And the journalist Hannon, what happened to him?"

"I understand he's written articles and a couple of books about the possibility of extraterrestrial life forms visiting earth, but of course he can't prove anything."

Suddenly there was a knock at the door. Curtis rose from his seat, walked across the room and opened the door. It was Price.

"Sorry to disturb you, but we've just received a call from CIA headquarters. We're to fly you to area 51."

"When?" asked Curtis angrily? He was getting frustrated at not being able to continue talking to Kidman and being flown from one place to the next at a moment's notice.

"Now, they want you there immediately."

"What about him?" he said quietly.

"We're to take care of him," said Price.

Curtis paused for a moment. He wondered what fate lay in store for Kidman and felt he should be treated better, then he walked back to the table and picked up the brown A4 envelope which Hoffman had sent him. He looked at Kidman, then made his way towards Price still waiting at the door. "You make sure no harm comes to him is that clear?" said Curtis looking straight at Price, but the military man just looked back at Curtis but made no reply. Knowing that his request would mean nothing, Curtis sighed and said quietly, "Okay, let's go."

chapter four
OUT OF THIS WORLD

November 23rd, 1963

Steve Curtis had travelled by private jet to Area 51. He'd managed to sleep for most of his journey, except for the last hour when he'd been reading the documents sent to him by James Hoffman. They made interesting reading, and it meant that more questions had to be answered. After receiving his identity card, Curtis walked into the elevator car, which descended to Saltzman's underground room. He began to think about the photographs that had been taken by Saltzman's orbiter as it passed over the Sinus Medii region of the moon. Had they revealed more detail about the object, or had sending a secret space probe to investigate been an expensive mistake? The elevator car stopped and the doors slid open. Curtis walked into the underground room with the documents inside the brown envelope in his hand.

"Mr Curtis, it's nice to see you again," said the very excited Vigo Saltzman. "I take it Mr Hoffman isn't joining us today?"

"No, he's had to stay in Dallas, and he'll be there for some time. If it hasn't escaped your notice, President Kennedy was murdered yesterday, Mr Saltzman, and the whole world happens to be in mourning over the event."

"Yes, yes, a terrible time for all of us, Mr Curtis. We have to make sure the communists don't take advantage of the situation."

"I'm sure there are many people who might take advantage of the situation if we're not careful. People who are a little closer to home, wouldn't you say?" said Curtis looking straight at Saltzman. He could sense no grief in the industrialist's voice over the loss of the president, and he realized he had to be on his guard more than ever before.

"Yes, well, would you like to come and join us, Mr Curtis? There's something of great importance you have to see."

Both men walked briskly across the room to join Colonel Gorman, Dave Rossi, and Professor Steiner. The professor had just finished pinning a sixteen by twelve inch photograph to a board which was resting on an easel.

"Gentlemen, if you'd like to gather round," said the professor.

Gorman, Rossi, and Curtis formed a semi-circle round the easel, and waited for Saltzman to reveal their findings. The industrialist stood on the left side of the easel, the professor on the right.

"Gentlemen," said Saltzman. "We have some startling news to give you. Our orbiter spacecraft has been a great success. In fact it has revealed more than we could have ever imagined, and when you see what I'm talking about you'll realize more than ever how important it is that we reach the moon first."

Curtis, Rossi, and Gorman, looked at each other, puzzled as to what this was all about. They all looked at the strange grainy image which meant very little to them, and all were anxious to know more.

"The photograph you're looking at gentlemen, has been processed here in our laboratories after receiving the transmissions from the lunar orbiter. Now, the spacecraft was traveling in a thirty mile orbit with a ten degree angle to the lunar surface when this photograph of the object was taken. Professor would you like to continue?"

"Thank you," said Steiner. "Now because we know the height and angle of our spacecraft, we can work out the height of our object using basic trigonometry. The horizon is less than ten miles away, so we have calculated that the height of the object stands approximately one mile high with a diameter of one and a half miles at its base."

Curtis, Gorman, and Rossi looked at one another in disbelief.

"What?" said Gorman. "Are you absolutely sure about this?"

"We most certainly are," said Steiner.

The professor picked up a twelve inch ruler and began to point out the light grey area extruding from the lunar surface.

"Gentlemen, if you look carefully at this area which we say has been calculated to be a mile high, you'll notice a series of dark lines cutting diagonally across the object."

Carefully Steiner pointed out the dark lines in the object with the ruler.

"Notice these lines go from left to right and right to left creating perfect hexagon shapes within the area."

"Just a minute," said Gorman. "These lines, are they caused by heat or some sort of erosion?"

"No Colonel, they are not. They're too perfect to be caused by erosion and no way have they been created by heat."

"So what are you saying?" said Rossi.

Saltzman then walked in front of the easel and faced the three men.

"Gentlemen, from the moment we looked upon the photographs given to Mr Curtis just over a year ago, we believed the Russians had discovered an alien spacecraft. It is our belief that this is not so."

Saltzman turned and faced the photograph. "We believe that what you are looking at is a complex framework which is covered in a transparent material. Now this material may be glass, or a kind of plastic, we're not sure. What is for sure, is that we are looking at large structure made by an intelligent mind."

There was total silence in the room as they stared at the photograph.

"Now hold on a minute, Vigo," said Gorman. "Are you trying to tell us that's some kind of building?"

"Or monument of some kind, Mr Gorman," said Saltzman in a loud excited voice.

"Monument to what?" asked Curtis.

"We don't know, but one thing is for sure, and that it is not a spaceship."

Curtis couldn't believe what he was hearing. "What do you base this on, Saltzman? A few dark lines on a grainy photograph tell you nothing."

"They're not lines on the photograph, Mr Curtis," said Steiner. "There's definite geometry in the image."

Gorman moved closer to the photograph and studied it. "If you're right professor, then this is the greatest discovery mankind has ever made."

"I know we're right Colonel," continued Steiner. "If you look at the overall shape of the structure, even in this poor quality enlargement, you'll notice it's a perfect dome."

The professor ran his pen around the outline of the sphere then began to point at the framework inside it once more.

"This framework is a wonderful piece of engineering. There's no way it can be anything else."

Curtis and Rossi approached the easel and examined the image. There was no doubt about it; there was a structure near the crater Ukert in the Sinus Medii region. The question was, who put it there, and for what purpose?

"How long do you reckon this sphere's been on the moon, professor?"

"I'm afraid to say that's one thing we have no knowledge of Steve. It could have been there hundreds of years, maybe thousands. It could have been there even since the beginning of time itself."

"You say it could be made of glass professor," added Rossi. "Surely it would have been smashed to pieces by now, because of meteor activity."

"Yes, you're quite right, but do remember that on the moon glass does have the structural strength of steel, but it would still receive some form of damage I must admit."

"Okay, so let's assume that this dome or whatever it is, has been put there recently," said Curtis. "Let's say in the past hundred years. Could it survive over that period of time?"

"Sure,"but....."

Before the professor could finish what he was saying, Gorman, still studying the print, interrupted. "How many people know about this?" he asked.

"What was that?" replied Curtis.

Gorman turned and looked at the rest of the group. "I said how many people know about this?"

"Just us," said Saltzman.

"We have to keep it that way for the time being. I don't think there's much point in discussing how long this dome has been on the moon, the fact is, it's there and we have to reach it before the Russians."

"They discovered this in the first place," said Rossi. "I wonder whether they've found out what it really is."

"The chances are that they have. Vigo, what's the plan of action you wish to take with this?"

"Well, N.A.S.A will obviously be sending their ranger spacecraft's to photograph the moon for possible landing sites. Now with luck they'll keep away from the Sinus Medii region and concentrate their efforts on more smoother and flatter areas of the lunar surface."

"Luck, I don't think you can bank on that," said Curtis. "If they're going to survey the moon for Apollo landing sites, I can't see how they're going to miss this."

There was silence amongst the group for a moment.

"I'm afraid N.A.S.A is going to have to know about it," said Rossi reluctantly.

"No, no," said Gorman raising his voice. "There are too many people involved. All it takes is for one individual to open his mouth and that's it."

"Maybe we're underestimating the N.A.S.A personnel," said Curtis. "Dave, you're training for a moon landing, do you think the astronauts could keep quiet if we told them what was at stake here?"

"Oh come on Steve," said Gorman. "Do you think all the technicians involved in the space programme could keep quiet for God's sake?"

Saltzman, doing his usual prancing back and forth suddenly stopped. "I have experts working for my company who have studied the moon for many years. Now I'm sure N.A.S.A will be calling on these people at some point in the near future for advice. I can call a meeting with them and tell them to suggest that N.A.S.A stay away from the Sinus Medii."

Gorman was not convinced. "On what grounds?"

"Well, we'd have to tell them that the area is too dangerous for a landing, and if a lunar module were to crash it could be catastrophic for N.A.S.A as an organization."

Gorman, still unsure, said, "I don't think they'll go for that."

Saltzman looked at the group of men standing around him. All of them were silent, wondering how they could keep their secret to themselves.

Saltzman, with no other ideas, said, "I don't see what else we can do. Do remember our spacecraft was in a thirty mile high orbit. The Apollo crafts will be twice that high, plus the fact they'll be looking for landing sites, not structures."

Gorman placed his hands over his face and gently rubbed his tired eyes.

"Well, we're just going to have to watch the Apollo programme very carefully," he said. "If the N.A.S.A astronauts find or photograph this dome, we're just going to have to find some way of discrediting it. The most important thing we have to do is keep quiet and work together, okay?" Each of them nodded in agreement, except for Curtis.

"I think if we've all agreed to do that, it's important that we should be on the level with each other every step of the way."

"What do you mean by that?" asked Gorman.

Curtis then opened the brown envelope and removed the documents inside.

"Well it seems to me that certain events in 1947 have been kept quiet Colonel. For instance, why weren't we told about the second alien?"

There was a silence for a moment.

"What second alien?" asked Saltzman.

"You mean you don't know about it?"

Curtis was surprised that Saltzman didn't seem to know anything about this.

"No, this is the first I have heard about it," he replied.

"Colonel Gorman, I've got documents here claiming that you know about the alien which was found by Colonel Kramer the day after you discovered the spacecraft."

"What do you mean second alien?" asked Saltzman. "Why haven't we been told about this Colonel?"

"Well Colonel?" asked Curtis.

Gorman walked towards one of the large sofas and sat down.

"Yes, it's true that a second alien was discovered. It was brought to one of the airbases under strict security, for medical attention. He was badly injured and was taken straight to the medical centre, where two surgeons, Dr James Starkey and Dr David Newton, fought to save his life. It was of utmost importance that we tried to save him. Imagine it, a man from another world in our hands, all the things we could learn if we could just keep him alive. The surgeons fought hard for six hours, while Colonel Kramer and I waited anxiously outside the operating room for their report," Gorman began the story of the second alien.

The sun began to set over the airbase as Colonel Kramer gazed out of the window of the medical centre. Never in his career had he been in a position that he was in now. For the first time the Americans were in possession of a living being from another world. There were so many questions the Colonel would want to ask the alien, but would he get the chance?

Gorman had just arrived and made his way towards Kramer.

"Hi Roy, how's things?"

"Oh I'm fine John. I've been here for hours; time seems to drag at moments like this."

There was quite a long silence as both men became lost in their thoughts about the incident. Then Kramer, longing to know more, asked, "What was it like John, discovering that thing out there?"

Gorman, recalling the night before, replied, "I didn't know what to think at first, I remember touching the thin metal of the craft and marvelling at its incredible strength. Then when I saw the alien inside, well I felt my whole life was about to change."

"I've got news for you; your life is going to change. From now on in you're in charge of this thing."

Once again there was a moment's pause as Gorman thought about what lay ahead of him.

"I wonder how long these beings have been visiting our world John, since the beginning of time, do you think?"

"Well if they have, they certainly haven't interfered in anything we've done," replied Gorman.

Just then the door opened and two security men entered and approached Kramer and Gorman.

"Colonel Kramer?"

"Yes."

"The defence secretary has arrived, sir."

"Right, let's go and meet him," replied Kramer.

Before they reached the door another security officer entered along with the Minister of Defence, Edward McClintock.

The six foot two Texan approached the two military men. He'd been ordered by the President to give the situation top priority and to have a full report at the White House within twenty four hours.

"Okay gentlemen, what do we have?" asked the Minister.

"Would you like to come with us, sir?" asked Kramer.

McClintock, Kramer and Gorman walked towards the operating theatre leaving the security men behind.

"Well, sir, within the last forty-eight hours the United States has come into possession of an extraterrestrial space vehicle and its two man crew. One of these aliens was killed and found at the controls of the craft by Colonel Gorman, the other found twelve hours later by myself. It was believed that this alien had tried to use some kind of escape pod to abandon the crippled craft, before it crashed into the desert."

"Where is the craft now?"

"It's at a maximum security base being examined by our scientists," said Gorman.

"Can this alien communicate with us?"

"Well he seemed to understand what we were saying when we were trying to help him, sir."

At that moment the door of the operating theatre opened and Dr Newton walked briskly towards the three men.

"Gentlemen, I don't know how long we have, but we've done all we can," said the doctor. "He has severe internal injuries and I'm afraid we have to fear the worst. If you want to try and communicate with him this will probably be the only chance you'll have."

Quickly the four men made their way into the operating theatre. Dr

Starkey was holding the alien's hand pleading with him to cling onto life. The alien was very pale and was struggling to breathe. It was clear that time was running out for the young astronaut. The alien turned his head slowly to the right and looked directly at McClintock.

Breaking loose from the doctor, the alien stretched out his hand towards the Secretary of State.

"Sir," said Newton. "I think it's you he wants to communicate with."

Nervously McClintock moved towards the operating table. Taking the alien by the hand he leaned forward trying to hear the words the dying man was trying to say. The alien took a deep breath and spoke these words: "SHARE YOUR WORLD OR YOU WILL DIE." Again he repeated the words, slowly closed his eyes, and passed away.

"Share your world or die?" repeated Curtis as Gorman finished telling his story. "What did he mean?"

"Well, I know what the Secretary of State thought the alien meant."

"Oh, what's that?"

"He took it as a threat."

Rossi unsure why the defence minister should think that way asked, "Why did he think it was a threat?"

"I'm afraid we had to believe that, they were the alien's final words just before he died. With nothing else to go on, we just couldn't take the risk."

Rossi wanted to know more. "Was there an autopsy?"

"Yes, it was quite amazing. It was found that the alien had the same skeletal structure as us. Two lungs, heart, liver, kidneys. However they had been genetically modified. What's more astonishing is that both aliens were exact replicas of each other."

Steiner looked at Saltzman and nodded. "This sounds like cloning to me."

"Yes, but it looks like these people have perfected it," said Curtis. "Cloning and genetically modifying their astronauts for what?"

Steiner felt there could be an explanation for this. "Well we know that long space flights would have a serious effect on bone and muscles. There's a chance that these people have been modified just for space flight, something we may have to do with our own astronauts one day.

"Good God," muttered Saltzman.

Steiner looked troubled as he thought about his time in Nazi Germany. "I've always been against the idea of cloning. I remember how a group of German scientists experimented with human cloning in 1943 using Jewish women for hosts. The results were too appalling to even talk about."

"That was the Nazis professor," said Gorman. "As Steve just said these aliens have perfected the technology."

"Yes, but at what cost?" replied Steiner sadly. "I wonder how many failures they had before they perfected this process."

"I guess that's the price every race has to pay for progress," said Rossi.

"Progress? If you had lived through what I saw in the nineteen forties, Mr Rossi, you would not call it progress."

"Well, there's nothing we can do until N.A.S.A put a man on the moon," said Gorman. "Once they've done that, I'll make sure that the moon programme is cut short so we can get on with our mission."

"And you have the power to do that?" asked Rossi.

"Not me personally, but the people I work for do."

Saltzman walked over to the easel and looked at the grainy photograph.

"It will seem like eternity for me before we launch our expedition," he said. "Just think of the advanced treasures that must be waiting for us in that dome, gentlemen. We must be the first to reach it. We must have that alien technology."

chapter five

REACH FOR THE MOON

February 2nd, 1973

It has been ten years since the discovery of the dome structure on the moon, which was accidentally photographed by a Russian lunar space probe. The 1960's ended with the United States of America achieving John Kennedy's goal of reaching the moon ahead of the Soviet Union. Neil Armstrong had taken his giant leap for mankind and the Genesis rock discovered, with the Apollo 15 mission. Gene Cernan and Harrison Schmitt were the last of the twelve men from earth to leave the lunar surface, and now all was set for the secret Apollo mission headed by American industrialist, Vigo Saltzman. His aim was to reach the dome which he believed contained advanced technology left behind by the extraterrestrial race which built the structure. Saltzman and the secret military group known as Majestic, believe that this race of beings could be those who tried to make contact with earth in 1947. If there is a connection between this race and the dome at Sinus Medii, then now will be the time for it to be confirmed.

Saltzman had risen from his bed just before sunrise. Taking his private car from the accommodation block at the space centre at Cape Kennedy, he drove himself down to the beach. Bringing the vehicle to a halt he switched off the engine and climbed out. Now a man in his mid-sixties, he looked out over the ocean and took a deep breath of the salty air. The sky seemed to be ablaze with fire as the morning sun rose over the Atlantic, bringing a new day to the east coast of Florida. The only sound that could be heard was the roar of waves crashing against the rocks, and the cry of seabirds flying over the cape. Then he turned and faced the rocket base. Silhouetted against the morning sunlight on launch pad 39B, stood Apollo 18, attached to the launch tower by nine umbilical arms. The three hundred and sixty three foot high rocket had been transported from the assembly building two days earlier by the enormous crawler vehicle. Final system checks were now being carried out by the mission controllers as fuel and electricity were being supplied to each stage. A thin layer of ice had started to form over the outer shell of the spacecraft, caused by the freezing cold temperatures of the liquid oxygen. Once mixed with the kerosene fuel, this liquid would produce the explosive power of seven point five million pound of thrust, hurtling the giant rocket skywards and into earth's orbit.

Saltzman tried to relax while the launch time crept ever closer. Unfortunately this moment came to an abrupt end, as the sound of an approaching car became louder as it sped towards him. A white, open top, Corvette sports car came to a halt close to him and C.I.A chief James Hoffman, now in his late sixties, climbed out and walked briskly towards him.

"Mr Hoffman, I didn't expect to see you at the launch."

"I'm afraid we've got some problems Vigo."

"What sort of problems?" asked an alarmed Saltzman.

"The Russians are preparing a rocket. Sergei Tarelkin reported they could be trying for a moon landing."

"When did he report this?"

"Yesterday."

"Oh my God," shouted an annoyed Saltzman. "Why the hell wasn't I informed earlier?"

"I had to be sure before I sent Curtis out there."

"Jesus," said Saltzman clenching his fist and hitting the roof of his car. "Are the Russians capable of landing a man on the moon?"

"Well, they've been testing their latest moon rocket for some time, but with some disastrous results."

"Well, let's hope this bastard's a disaster."

"Curtis and Tarelkin are going to try and stop the launch as soon as possible, but it won't be easy."

"How the hell are they going to do that?"

"I'm leaving it to them," said Hoffman sounding confident. He knew if any men could stop the Russian launch it was Curtis and the Russian rebel.

"Have we any idea when they're planning to launch?"

"No. "Apparently we are in luck. The weather in Kazakhstan is playing havoc. A storm is covering the entire area, and they won't be able to launch anything for another twenty four hours."

"Good," said Saltzman with some relief. "That gives us a day's start at least. We can be on the moon, take whatever is inside the dome, and destroy the place before the Russians get near."

"You're forgetting something," said Hoffman knowing that Saltzman had overlooked an important matter. "Our President knows nothing about the real reason for this mission. Don't forget we told him and everyone else that we were going in search of what we believed could be a rare mineral on the lunar surface."

"Of course we had to tell them that. "If ever the real reason got out the whole world would want to know what we'd discovered, never mind the President."

"Yes, and there's something else you may have overlooked. Assuming the Russian Premier knows nothing and there's a damn good chance he doesn't, his scientists could destroy the Apollo command module on its return trip to earth."

"Damn," said an angry Saltzman. "If they did that we'd have to make up some story that an accident had happened on our spacecraft, or risk starting world war three."

"That's right," said Hoffman nodding his head in agreement.

"And you know what that would mean."

"Yes, don't tell me, N.A.S.A. would be grounded. There'd be no more missions to the moon and possibly no Skylab. There's no way we'd be allowed to return to the lunar surface and study the dome further."

"So there's only one alternative and that's to stop the Russian rocket from getting off the ground."

Saltzman nodded. "Yes that's the only way," he said. "I hope Curtis knows what he's doing."

"He'll have a plan, don't worry about that. Once he reaches the Russian cosmodrome he'll make his way to the launch site."

"What in hell," screamed Saltzman. "Are you trying to tell me Curtis is going to just walk into the Baikanour rocket base?"

"No, he's going to fly in using a Russian Mig 23 fighter plane."

"Can he fly one?"

Hoffman laughed. "He should be able to; after all he stole it from a Russian air base so your company could steal its radar technology."

"Well, I'll be damned," said the surprised industrialist. "I was told a Russian pilot who defected to the west had landed that aircraft on American soil two years ago."

"No, that's the story we told the media," said Hoffman. "We're going to use the Mig to get into the rocket base's air field. There's a team of our engineers working on the plane right now at our base in Turkey. I'll let you know when I've any more information to give you."

Hoffman wouldn't say any more than that. He'd learnt from bitter experience that it was in the best interests of his agents that any plan of action should not be discussed with anyone.

He turned and started to walk back to his car. As he did he called out to Saltzman, "Get Apollo launched and leave the Russian rocket to us."

Climbing into the white Corvette he slammed the door shut. With a deep drone the sports car's engine fired up and roared away, its back wheels spinning on the dirt track. Quickly Saltzman did the same. He climbed into his car and headed back to the suiting up room to give Rossi his final instructions. The three Apollo astronauts had been preparing for launch for the last two hours. The vehicle that would take them to the launch pad had already been driven to the side entrance of the suiting up room. There were no press or media present. Flying to the moon had become routine and public and TV interest had dwindled. This of course would be in this mission's favour as there were fewer people asking questions. This didn't bother Rossi. The usual razzamatazz that went with a rocket launch didn't appeal to him anyway, plus the fact that this was the most important expedition to the moon, and he was commander. This meant more to him than being the first man to set foot on our celestial partner.

A technician carefully pulled a communications cap over Rossi's head.

"Is that okay, Dave?"

"No problem," said the commander turning to his left. He glanced over at his long-time friend, command module pilot Andrew Wilson.

"You okay Andy?" asked Rossi in a loud confident voice.

"Sure thing, Dave," replied the thirty eight year old Texan.

Wilson had been first in the suiting up room that morning and was now having the high-strength polycarbonate helmet placed over his head.

"Can you just tilt your head back Andrew?" asked Alan Grant, one of the senior technical team. Grant had helped prepare Apollo crew members for launch since the late 1960's. He and his wife Faith had become close friends with the Wilson family ever since Andrew joined N.A.S.A. in 1965. Grant turned the helmet forty five degrees locking it into position on the sealing ring which was attached to Wilson's spacesuit. Unlike the helmets worn on the Mercury and Gemini missions that were closely fitted and moved with the astronauts head, the Apollo helmet was fixed which meant the astronaut could move his head inside it. A life support tank, connected to the spacesuit through a metre long hose, supplied Wilson with oxygen while extracting carbon dioxide as the astronaut exhaled. Tilting his head backwards and forwards and from side to side checking the helmet and communications cap for comfort, Wilson looked towards Rossi. Clenching both fists he raised his arms and gave the thumbs up to his commander in a gesture to say that he was ready. Rossi then turned towards Stuart Martin, who, like Wilson, was almost ready for the events that lay ahead. Apart from being the lunar module co-pilot, Martin was also a geologist. Born in Santa Rita, New Mexico, he graduated from Western High School, Silver City, receiving a science degree from the California Institute of Technology, before moving on to Harvard University in 1965, where he received a doctorate in Geology.

He and Rossi would fly the lunar module, code named Europa, to the surface of the moon. Then using the lunar rover the men would drive the rest of the journey to the glass dome. There they would retrieve as much alien technology and information as possible and bring it back to earth. That was the plan but Rossi sat wondering whether the mission would be that easy. After all they would only be able to bring back a small amount because of the size of their space craft.

At that moment Saltzman walked into the suiting up room. Without acknowledging anyone else he walked straight towards Rossi. "All set to go, Dave?" he asked, giving the commander a gentle slap on the back.

"Yeah, I think we'll all set," he said confidently as he glanced once again at Wilson and Martin. Alan Grant walked across the room to the two men. He appreciated that Saltzman was in charge of the mission but to walk into the suiting up room was totally against the standards of previous space missions.

"You know you're not supposed to enter this room, Mr Saltzman," said Grant with some annoyance. "All forms of contamination could be brought in from outside, you do know that don't you?"

Saltzman turned slowly to Grant. "Listen, if I want to talk to my commander I will. I don't need permission from you or anyone else. I'm head of this mission and maybe you'd like to remember that."

Not being frightened easily Grant stood his ground. "Well that's fine with me. I'd just like you to remember that if any of these astronauts fall ill during the flight after you've breathed your germs over them, this mission will be aborted. Maybe you'd like to remember that."

"Hey come on guys," said Rossi. "Things are always a little tense before lift-off, let's just give one another a break, okay?"

After a moment's silence, Saltzman repented. "Yes, well I'm sorry, but could you give me a minute with Dave?"

"Okay, but make it quick," said Grant politely as he moved away to check on the other two astronauts. Saltzman looked around, making sure that no one was listening. "How are things, Dave, are you ready to go?"

"You've already asked me that. Yes, we're ready to go," said Rossi knowing full well that Saltzman hadn't come to wish him bon voyage. He could tell by the sound of his voice there was something troubling him. "Vigo, why don't you tell me the real reason you're here?"

Saltzman looked at Rossi nervously wondering what reaction the astronaut would have once he was told the Russians had a moon rocket ready for launch.

"Dave, we believe that the Russians are going to try and reach the dome before us."

Rossi was shocked to hear this news.

"Are the Russians capable of landing a manned craft?" he asked in a worried voice.

"We don't know," replied Saltzman quietly. "But with so much at stake they could try it."

"When are they launching?" asked Rossi, concerned for himself and his crew.

"As soon as they can, but thankfully bad weather has halted their launch time. At this moment Steve Curtis is making his way to their rocket base, hoping to stop the launch."

"Hoping? What if he fails?"

Saltzman looked at the astronaut but said nothing. Rossi sighed deeply. "Well, let's hope to God Curtis stops that rocket or we're all in trouble. I'll tell Andrew and Stuart once we're out of earth orbit."

"I don't think you should tell them," said Saltzman nervously.

Rossi turned quickly to face Saltzman. "What do you mean?" he replied angrily. "Listen, Andrew and Stuart are my crew. I don't believe in taking men on any mission without them knowing the full implications of what they're up against."

"Yes, but ...."

"But nothing. That's the way it's going to be," snapped Rossi.

Saltzman took a deep breath. "Okay, Dave, you play it your way."

He stopped and looked at the astronaut, and wondered what lay ahead for Rossi and his crew. Holding out his hand, he said, "Good luck, Dave, take care." He paused and looked at Rossi once more then turned and started to walk away.

"Hey, Saltzman." The industrialist stopped and turned towards Rossi. "I hope whatever we find up there is going to be worth it."

"It will be Commander, it will be."

Rossi watched Saltzman turn and walk out the door. The astronaut thought for a moment, "Maybe it would have been better for all of us if the Russians had never found that thing, then neither country could take possession of its contents."

"Let's get this helmet on, Dave. Andrew and Stuart are ready to go," said Grant, wakening Rossi from his day dreaming. Slowly the technician lowered the polycarbonate helmet onto the locking ring of the commander's spacesuit. Turning it forty five degrees he heard the slight click as it locked into position. He picked up the life support container and slowly turned on the oxygen.

"That enough air, Dave?"

Rossi gave the thumbs up gesturing that everything was fine, then Grant handed Rossi the container. The rear door of the building opened and a security officer walked in shouting, "Okay guys, we're ready."

Dave Rossi stood erect and proud as he walked to the exit door where he, Wilson, and Martin would climb into the transport vehicle that would take them to the launch pad. There was no great send off for this man and his crew like there was for Apollo astronauts that had gone before, just a friendly slap on the back from Grant was all they got. Security was so tight, not even Rossi's wife Jackie was allowed to say goodbye. Yet this was the big one. A moon mission where man's greatest dream could come true: to retrieve artefacts from another world that belonged to an alien race.

As the three astronauts were being transported to the launch pad, Steve Curtis was already in his flying suit being briefed by Colonel Joe McCarthy at the U.S air base in Turkey. It was late afternoon and Curtis was planning to make his flight so he could arrive at the Baikonur Cosmodrome in the middle of the night.

"Steve," said McCarthy. "Our weather people tell us that the dust storm in Kazakhstan isn't clearing, so the Russians are still grounded."

"Okay, well that's good news for us. The longer they're in trouble the better. Is the Mig ready yet?"

"Yeah, it arrived six hours ago. I hope Saltzman doesn't mind us using the Mig you stole for his company."

"Yeah, well I'm afraid if he wants this job doing he's got to help us to help him," said Curtis as he zipped up the Russian flight suit.

"Right let's go and check out that Mig."

The two men made their way through the door of the briefing room and headed down the corridor towards the hangar where the Mig 23 had been prepared.

"What do you think the Russians are planning to do?" asked McCarthy.

"It's hard to say. They could try to reach the moon before we do and claim whatever mineral there is."

McCarthy knew nothing about the dome. He, like everyone else, had been told that Apollo eighteen's mission was to investigate a rare mineral which Saltzman believed to be in the Sinus Medii region of the moon. Although he played along with what Curtis was saying, McCarthy had his suspicions that something was being kept quiet, but the colonel was a dedicated military man who knew security when he saw it, so he didn't question the C.I.A agent.

The two men walked through a door at the end of the corridor which led into the hangar. There in front of them stood the Mig 23; four meters high and sixteen meters in length, with its significant swing wing feature. The Soviet warbird was ahead of its time in aircraft technology, making it a formidable adversary to the U.S air force.

"It's been a long time since I flew this plane," said Curtis.

"Stole it you mean, right from under their noses I'm led to believe," replied McCarthy.

Curtis turned to the Colonel and smiled. "Well if the Russians are going to leave their aircraft unguarded, what do they expect?"

Curtis began to walk around the aircraft anticlockwise, first checking that the rectangular box air-intake was free from any debris. McCarthy watched Curtis as the ace pilot carefully examined the leading-edge of the port wing. He slowly ran his hand along this section, checking for any damage the Mig may have received in the two years in which it had been in the possession of Saltzman aerospace. The wings were at full spread, giving the aircraft a forty five foot, ten inch wingspan. This would enable the Mig to use shorter take-off and landing runways while carrying a payload of heavy weapons. During the flight, the pilot would be able to change the angle of the swing wing craft to seventy two degrees enabling it to reach a speed of Mach 2.35. He continued to work his way around to the trailing edge of the wing, once again gently feeling for any damage to the ailerons and flaps.

"We've taking good care of her you know," said McCarthy.

"I can see that," replied Curtis making his way to the rear of the long tubular fuselage. In front of the engine afterburner was the small tapered belly fin in its retractable position. In flight this fin would be extended to give greater stability to the aircraft at high speed. Moving around to the starboard side of the Mig, Curtis repeated the flight checks before walking along side the aircraft's long nose section. This housed the Sapfir-23ML J-band multi-mode radar. This sophisticated piece of avionics provided the pilot with a picture which was projected onto a head up display screen, rather than using a radar scope. Curtis made his way back to McCarthy.

"Well Colonel, she looks in good shape."

"It's a good aircraft Steve, we've learnt a lot from her."

Curtis checked his watch. "It won't be long before the launch of Apollo 18. I'd better be going."

"Okay, I'll get up to the control tower," replied the Colonel. "Oh just before you go, I thought this might be of some help."

McCarthy reached into his top pocket and pulled out a piece of paper which had been folded into quarters, then handed it to Curtis. He opened it wondering what it could be.

"It's a map of the entire cosmodrome," said McCarthy. "We thought you might find it useful."

"Sure it's useful. How the hell did you get a plan of the Russian base?" asked Curtis gratefully.

"You have your secrets Steve, we have ours," smiled the Colonel.

He looked at the layout of the complex very carefully. The map showed the R7 launch pads to the west of the airstrip where he was planning to land, with tracking stations to the east. He noticed the nitrogen and liquid oxygen production plants to the south, and slowly a plan of action began to form in the agent's mind. Curtis looked up at McCarthy as he folded the map and placed it in the top pocket of his flight suit.

"Thanks Colonel, that's a big help," he said gratefully. "Okay I'm out of here."

Both men turned and walked towards the front section of the Mig. As they approached the aircraft, Curtis gazed at the twenty three millimetre GSH-23L twin barrel gun mounted in the belly of the fuselage.

"It's fully loaded Steve just in case you need to use it," smiled McCarthy.

"Thanks but I'll try not to," he said as he climbed the ladder towards the cockpit.

Curtis's plan was to land the Mig at the cosmodrome's airfield in full view of the Russian personnel. He thought with everyone's mind firmly on the launch of the rocket, an extra Mig landing at the base would go unquestioned. Reaching the top of the ladder, he took the pilot's helmet off the seat and climbed in. Gently lowering himself into position, he placed the crash helmet over his head then gazed at the flight panel in front of him. Familiarizing himself with the controls, Curtis felt confident that the aircraft would perform well. He checked the seatbelt was secure before placing the face mask round his nose and mouth and clipping it to the inside of the helmet. Flicking the switches to their start up positions a series of lights began to illuminate the control panel. Computer, navigation systems, head up display, were all working perfectly. Then pressing the ignition button the air intake fans on the Soyuz, Khachaturov R-35-300 turbojet began to rotate, increasing revolution by the second till finally the roar of the engine echoed around the hangar. Curtis lifted his right hand and gestured to McCarthy that he was ready to move out. The Colonel made his way out of the hangar and headed for the control tower. Curtis increased the throttle and the Mig 23 began to roll forward. The Russian fighter slowly picked up speed as the pilot began to taxi out of the hangar and down to the end of the main runway.

Curtis looked upwards at a clear night sky. He began to realize that this would probably be the most important mission of his life. The decisions and actions that he would make in the next four to six hours would be crucial if the Americans were to possess whatever artefacts lay in the dome on the moon. As the agent began to line up the Mig at the end of the runway, McCarthy contacted him on the radio.

"Steve this is control. You're clear to go when you're ready."

"Thanks Colonel. As soon as I take off no more radio calls please. It's imperative no one hears our transmissions."

"Okay Steve, good luck."

Curtis pushed the throttle and the Mig surged forward. The roar of its engine could be heard across the base as the pilot was pushed back into his seat. Reaching take off speed Curtis gently pulled the joystick towards him and the nose of the Mig began to lift. As the aircraft began to gain altitude, Curtis pushed a small lever located on the right hand side of the control panel and instantly the undercarriage retracted.

Once the Mig reached thirty thousand feet, Curtis activated the two hydraulic wing sweep motors, which were driven separately by a control booster system within the fuselage. He first glanced out of the left-hand side of the cockpit canopy and then to the right, watching the aircraft's swing wing slowly retracting to an angle of seventy degrees.

Once in this position the pilot slowly opened the throttle reaching an air speed of Mach 2. Gently pressing the keys on the small computer in front of him,

Curtis punched the co-ordinates into the flight navigation system and the Mig 23 began to turn east towards the Russian boarder. "Next stop Baikanour," he thought as the aircraft headed off over the Caspian Sea.

At Cape Kennedy the crew of Apollo 18 sat patiently waiting for the final minutes to tick away before lift-off. Dave Rossi, sitting in the left hand seat of the three man capsule, looked across at his two colleagues.

"Okay guys, won't be long now," he said with great confidence in his voice.

"It's the moment I've been waiting for all my life," said Stuart Martin enthusiastically.

"Ever since I was a kid growing up in the Colorado Mountains, looking through my dad's telescope, I've longed to walk on the moon."

"Well, here's your big moment," said Andrew Wilson, "and what a moment it is."

Wilson paused and thought for a moment about what the other two astronauts would find in the alien dome. He turned his head and looked towards Rossi and Martin.

"I envy the two of you, good luck to both of you," he said with great sincerity.

Wilson would be orbiting the moon in the command module code named Titan while his fellow astronauts were exploring the extraterrestrial dome which Wilson would have loved to have seen for himself. Although this opportunity had not been destined for him, Wilson was a true professional and dedicated pilot. He was honoured and proud to be part of such a mission that he was determined to fulfil his responsibilities impeccably.

In the control room at Cape Kennedy, Saltzman's team, a carefully selected group from his scientific and engineering empire, monitored the data coming into their computers. Behind the group stood the industrialist himself, taking full control of the mission. He smiled with pride as he looked at the Saturn 5 rocket which was projected onto a large TV screen at the front of the control room. Finally sitting down, he gently moved his chair forward into his desk and closer to the microphone which would put him in direct contact with all the flight controllers.

"Apollo 18 flight controllers, could I have your attention please?" said Saltzman looking up at the screen with pride. "Gentlemen, I want you all to look at the rocket on that screen."

All the flight controllers looked up from their computers and gazed at the Saturn 5 looming large on the screen in front them.

"For many years archaeologists have been discovering remnants of civilisations that have been lost for centuries. They've uncovered cities lying beneath the deserts and vegetation of our jungles. We have retrieved artefacts left behind by some of the greatest races that have ever lived. But today we embark on what is perhaps the greatest and most exciting expedition mankind has ever undertaken; to explore a structure left by a race and beings from another world. We're not sure what our astronauts will find, but we wish them God speed. This mission must not fail. If we do, then another country will not."

Saltzman was silent for a moment, allowing his team to think about what he'd said. Then he sat upright and with a loud and confident voice said, "Right gentleman, let's go to the moon."

The launch controllers went back to studying their instrument panels and data again, checking the pressure of the Saturn's fuel tanks and its life support systems. Then Professor Steiner entered the control room. He knew the launch was getting very close, so the German scientist walked to the rear of the building, distracting none of the technicians as he passed them.

As he approached Saltzman he held out his hand to the industrialist. "Good luck," he said quietly. "You've waited a long time for this moment."

"No Gerhard, we've waited a long time."

The professor smiled back, but he looked uneasy. Saltzman sensed something was wrong.

"Gerhard, what's the problem?"

"Nothing, nothing," he said. "I'm fine Vigo, I'm fine."

"Come on, this is our moment," said Saltzman. "Let's launch this rocket together."

Then with a strong voice of authority he addressed his team. "Apollo 18 controllers. Give me a go or no go for launch.

"Booster?"

In sequence each controller responded.

"We're go, flight."

Saltzman continued running through the technical list. "Retro?"

"Go."

"F.i.d.o."

"We're go here, flight."

"Guidance?"

"We're go."

"Surgeon?"

The flight Surgeon gazed at his monitors checking the blood pressure and heart rate of each astronaut. Satisfied at their conditions he replied, "Go."

"EECOM?"

"Go."

"G.N.C?"

"Go."
"Telmu?"
"Go."
"Control?"
"Go."
"Procedure?"
"Go."
"INCO?"
"Go."
"F.A.O?"
"Go."
"Network?"
"Go."
"Recovery?"
"Go."
"Cap com?"
"Go."

After a moment's silence Saltzman smiled and thought to himself. "We're ready." He then sat up, took a deep breath and said, "Apollo 18 we're all go for launch."

The three astronauts inside the command module looked at each other.

"This is our moment guys," said Rossi. "Let's go and shake hands with another race."

The final countdown then began.

"Twenty, nineteen, eighteen, seventeen, sixteen."

Saltzman looked at the large screen at the front of the control room, not once flinching or looking away.

"Fifteen, fourteen, thirteen."

The flight Surgeon, studying his instrument panel, noticed the heart rate of each astronaut beginning to rise slightly as the moment for launch approached.

"Twelve, eleven, ten, nine, eight, ignition sequence starts."

At that moment the five huge engines on stage one ignited.

The kerosene and liquid oxygen was being forced through the fuel pumps at a rate equal to a hundred diesel locomotives working in perfect synchronization. The flames from the engines rose upwards engulfing the four stabiliser fins located at the base of the first stage, before being sucked back beneath the rocket by a massive vacuum. As the giant rocket shook, the thin layer of ice which had formed around its outer skin began to fracture into millions of pieces and fall to the ground. Thousands of gallons of water forced through jet sprays stationed around the launch pad were activated, causing great plumes of steam which mixed with the smoke and flames of the rocket engines. Then the mighty vehicle rose two inches, and the four hold down arms which held the Saturn steady swung backwards. The nine umbilical arms and their fuel injector tubes disconnected simultaneously and swung ninety degrees to the side allowing the giant Saturn 5 to rise majestically from the launch pad.

"We have lift-off!" called out the flight controller.

Saltzman slowly slid his chair backwards and then stood up, watching the rocket leave the launch tower. Inside the tiny capsule, Rossi, Martin, and Wilson with their eyes glued to the instrument panel, calmly reported the status of the rocket back to the control room on the ground.

"We have lift-off seventeen minutes past the hour," reported Rossi.

As the mighty Saturn 5 surged skywards the Apollo Commander continued to report to the flight control.

"This is eighteen, we are now pitching and our trim is good. Our gimbals are good. Velocity on the line," he said as the G. forces pressed down on him and his colleagues.

"Course, right on line," said Wilson as he watched the gimbals and gyros slowly revolving on the control panel as the vehicle was guided onto its correct course. As the incredible weight of the rocket became lighter due to the fuel being burnt at hundreds of gallons per second, the vehicle soon reached its escape velocity. Rossi watched his instrument gauges with one hundred percent concentration. Stretching out his right hand he flipped open a Perspex safety flap, revealing a switch beneath it.

"Switching E.O.S to manual," he said as he flicked the switch. Immediately the five engines on stage one shut down. The exploding bolts which anchored this section of the rocket to the instrument coiler and upper stages exploded simultaneously. Thruster rockets on the second stage ignited pulling the vehicle clear of stage one, which slowly began to fall, toppling back into the earth's atmosphere. The five engines on the second stage ignited, sending the rocket higher into orbit.

Rossi stretched out his right hand again and pressed the button marked, 'L.E.S motor fire'. Instantly the solid rocket engine ignited on the escape tower. This was connected to a shield that covered the capsule on the command module, and immediately both components were jettisoned away from the space vehicle.

"Tower gone," said Rossi, and the three astronauts were now able to see through the windows of the capsule. Back at control, Saltzman was now doing his usual pacing up and down the room. The lift-off was going to plan, so he allowed his team to concentrate hard on what they were doing, rather than him interfering and giving orders, which at times he was inclined to do.

The capsule communicator, Frank Gregg, watching his instrument panel, was now aware that stage two, which was now three hundred and sixty seconds into its burn time, was ready to be jettisoned.

"Eighteen, this is control. Prepare for staging," said Gregg.

The exploding bolts which anchored stage two to its upper section detonated. Like the first stage, it separated gracefully and fell away from what remained of the Saturn, and instantly the S.B.4 engine burst into life on the final stage, putting the vehicle into its correct orbit.

"We have ignition on stage three," reported Rossi as his eyes continued to race back and forth across the control panel. The S.B.4 had a burn time of one hundred and sixty five seconds, so all three astronauts sat watching the clock carefully. On the ground Gregg was also watching the timer.

"Eighteen, S.B.4 cut off at twelve minutes thirty four seconds."

"Roger," replied Rossi. "Coming up on twelve minutes thirty four."

As the clock approached the cut-off time Rossi prepared to press the button which would cut the stage three engine.

"Five, four, three, two, one, shut down."

He pressed the button and instantly the engine stopped. The Apollo crew, along with the flight technicians on the ground, checked their computers and instrument panels. The spacecraft was in correct orbit with a speed of twenty five thousand mile per hour.

"Congratulations everyone," said Saltzman from across the control room. "I want to know when the crew is ready for T.L.I." He put his hand on Steiner's shoulder.

"Professor, it's time you and I had a drink."

Both men turned and headed out of the control room. Saltzman opened a door leading to a small office.

"After you, Professor."

Steiner walked pasted Saltzman who now had a smile of great pride and satisfaction on his face. They entered the room and sat at a desk facing each other. Saltzman opened the bottom drawer on the right side of the desk and pulled out two whisky glasses and a bottle of Scotch. Removing the top from the bottle he slowly began to pour the drink for Steiner.

"That's enough for me, thank you, Vigo."

As Saltzman stop pouring he handed the glass to the Professor. Still smiling with pride he said, "Did you ever think professor, back in the nineteen forties when you were helping Von Braun build the V2 rockets for Hitler that your efforts would all lead to this?"

Steiner took a sip of whisky. "No Vigo, I didn't think of it at all," he said.

The professor still looked troubled about something and Saltzman could see it.

"Gerhard, what's wrong?"

After a moment's silence the German rocket scientist looked towards Saltzman.

"Vigo, what are you really hoping to find in that dome or, more to the point, what would you like to find?"

With both hands clasped round his whisky glass, Saltzman leaned forward.

"You know full well want I want, the alien technology, of course. Knowledge beyond anything that we possess. Just think of it, when they bring it back to earth my corporation will analyse it, reproduce it, and the United States of America will be more advanced than any other country in the world. Our children's education will benefit. American industry will be streets ahead of everyone else, leaving the balance of power in our favour."

The professor looked down at the floor, disappointed in Saltzman's attitude. He knew the industrialist was a hard American businessman whose patriotism to his country was second to none, but Steiner had hoped for a little more compassion.

"Yes, the United States will no doubt reap the benefit," he said, "but what about the rest of the world, Vigo. What about the Third World and the poorer nations. Will starving children around the world benefit from such knowledge?"

Saltzman pushed his chair backwards, stood up, and walked around to the side of the desk. With his back to the professor and in a heartless voice he said, "I don't work for the third world, and neither do you professor. I serve my country, and I serve it with great pride."

Steiner shook his head. "I wasn't questioning your patriotism Vigo, but I am questioning your responsibility."

Saltzman faced the Professor. "God damn, don't you ever question my responsibility," he said with great annoyance. "I've always been responsible for my actions. My corporation has provided this country with some of the finest aircraft, rocket and computer technology ever seen."

"Yes, caring for your own country, Vigo, and your country alone," said Steiner.

Saltzman was furious at what the professor was saying. He stormed towards him, as he did so the Professor stood up quickly. Both men stood eyeball to eyeball.

"You hypocritical bastard," shouted the industrialist. "How dare you lecture me about caring for my own country? Where were your responsibilities when you were building Hitler's V weapons, and blasting the hell out of London? Were you caring about other people then? Did you care about young American soldiers when the Germans were gunning them down on the beaches of Europe? Were you concerned about anybody else but yourself? God damn there was no other country on this fucking earth that wanted to rule the world more than you damn Germans."

"Yes, yes, and where did it get us Vigo? It got us nowhere," replied Steiner. "We had the biggest army, finest battle ships, rockets, everything. We were more advanced than anyone, but we still could not win the war. We were hated by the rest of the world for what we did, and we still are by some people. Any country that uses military might to achieve its aims makes far too many enemies. If the United States aren't careful they'll suffer the same fate as we did."

Both men looked at each other saying nothing for a moment, and then the door of the office opened. It was one of the flight technicians.

"Mr Saltzman, Apollo 18 is go for T.L.I."

"Thank you, we'll be out in a moment."

Saltzman looked at Steiner. "Well, Professor?"

He stormed out of the room leaving Steiner lost in his thoughts. Saltzman quickly made his way to his desk and sat down.

"Eighteen, this is cap-com, you're go for T.L.I," said Gregg.

Then Rossi's voice came over the radio, "Copy that control, we are go for translunar insertion. Saltzman swivelled his chair to the right, and noticed Steiner slowly making his way to the rear of the control room. Looking as if he had given up on the mission, he sat down near a window and looked out, turning away from the events that were now happening.

In the Apollo capsule Rossi, Wilson, and Martin ignited the S.B 4 engine. With a terrific roar of thrust, the spacecraft was suddenly catapulted out of earth's gravitational pull at the speed of a rifle bullet. Martin lent forward a little in his seat and looked out of the command module window. The earth began to slowly move out of view as the velocity of the spacecraft shot the three astronauts out of earth orbit and on course for the moon. As Apollo 18 began its quarter of a million mile journey, Steve Curtis, flying the Mig 23, began his descent to the airstrip at the Baikanour Cosmodrome. Moving the control lever to adjust the angle of the wings for landing, Curtis was concerned that he had no contact from the air field.

"Surely they've picked me up on their radar by now," he thought to himself. "Why aren't they making any contact?"

He had no time to think too long about this problem as the Mig, which was now on a slow descent, cut thought the thin clouds giving Curtis a clear view of the runway lights in the distance. The storm that had stopped the Russians from launching their rocket had abated, and Curtis knew that the countdown would begin again. Throttling back the Mig to its landing speed of one hundred and forty knots, Curtis lowered the undercarriage and applied the air brakes. On the final approach, at a height of approximately two thousand feet, he could see the base lit up below him. Still there was no contact from the control tower as the Mig 23 crossed the threshold lights and touched down on the runway. The aircraft's speed reduced as Curtis shut off the throttle and deployed a parachute which opened from the rear of the fuselage. He had a brief moment to glance quickly across the area before turning the Mig off the runway. Lights in the buildings and hangars, and road lamps lit up the entire complex, and everything seemed to be very quiet. Apart from the odd military vehicle moving around the area, there was very little activity.

Curtis taxied the aircraft towards an open area in front of two large hangars where two other Mig 23's were lined up side by side. One was fully armed and ready for take-off, while four air frame technicians worked on the second aircraft. He brought his Mig to a halt, alongside the other two, and then shut down the aircraft's engine. Opening the canopy and releasing the seat belt, he gently pushed himself upright in the cockpit. Immediately one of the aircrew placed a ladder alongside the cockpit in order for Curtis to climb down. Carefully stepping onto the ladder he began his descent, keeping the visor of the helmet down to conceal his face.

"Spasibo," said Curtis confidently, which meant 'thank you' in Russian. He then turned and deliberately walked within yards of the rest of the ground crew who were still working on the second Mig. He raised his hand to acknowledge the Russian engineers as he walked past them. He thought the best way to not arouse suspicion was to act as normally as he possibly could.

Curtis walked calmly towards one of the hangars. Slowly he lifted the visor of the helmet and looked around for other airbase personnel. There wasn't much to see, but in the distance he could hear the voice of the launch controller over the base's speaker system giving the count down for the rocket. Checking that no one was watching him he ran along the outside of the hangar. He stopped and removed his helmet, throwing it behind some bushes. Taking the map of the base given to him by McCarthy from his top pocket, Curtis began to study it.

"Okay, let's reach the liquid oxygen and fuel complex," he thought to himself.

Placing the map in his top pocket, he headed back to the three Mig fighters where the ground crew was now fuelling the second Mig. He noticed that the first Mig had two air to air missiles mounted beneath its wings. These weapons were solid fuel type with a range of about fifteen kilometres.

"They resemble the American sidewinders," he thought. "Well, we steal their weapons, so I guess they have a right to steal ours."

The inboard missiles mounted under the fuselage were solid fuel RS-2U type, with a range of seven to eight kilometres which were guided by radar beam. They were an old design but nevertheless pretty lethal. Curtis turned and began to walk towards the hangar. As he approached he saw a UAZ 469 Russian military jeep just inside the main door way.

"Good I can use that."

As he entered the building he could hear voices echoing from the far side of the hangar, but couldn't see anyone. He reached the front of the jeep and lifted up the hood. Not having the keys, Curtis would have to hot wire the ignition to start the vehicle before driving to the fuel complex. Leaning over the engine he began to look for the wires that he could use to start the jeep. Suddenly the hood slammed hard down on his back. He moaned in agony as if someone had thrust a knife in the base of his spine. Then, as the hood flew open again, Curtis felt a large hand grab him round the back of the collar. With great force he was thrown backwards and sent tumbling to the floor of the hangar. Dazed and in some pain he shook his head and looked up. Standing over him were two Russian security men, one to his right, the other to the left. The one on the right who had pinned him to the engine was about six foot four in height and was about one hundred and forty nine pounds of muscle.

"Get up," said the Russian in a deep cold voice.

Curtis slowly rose to his feet, gently rubbing the base of his spine.

"My name is Aton Zhukov. Get in the rear of the vehicle, now."

Curtis walked slowly passed the two men and climbed onto the back seat of the jeep. Zhukov made his way round to the far side of the jeep and sat next to Curtis, while the other officer climbed into the driver's seat.

"Please don't give us any trouble," said the Russian, calmly thrusting a revolver into Curtis's side. "Make one move and it will be your last."

The driver started the jeep and drove quickly out of the hangar and towards the south east side of the base. Curtis realized that if he were locked in a prison cell, he wouldn't have time to stop the rocket from being launched, and that could be disastrous for the Apollo crew. As the Russian pressed the gun into Curtis's side a little harder, the American knew this wasn't the time or place to try anything. He decided to wait till they reached their destination before making his move.

Meanwhile the Apollo crew was preparing to dock the command module Titan with the lunar module Europa. The three astronauts, Wilson, Rossi, and Martin, made final instrumentation checks. This was a crucial stage of the mission, and all three astronauts were eager to negotiate this procedure with as much precision as possible.

"Okay, guys, all set," said Rossi.

"Okay, Dave, all set for separation and docking," replied Wilson.

In the control room at Cape Kennedy, Saltzman and his team were listening to the transmissions from the spacecraft.

"Cap-com, give our crew the go-ahead to proceed," said Saltzman, who was keen to press on with the mission. With his mind firmly on the moon landing, and retrieving whatever lay within the glass dome, the last thing concerning him were procedures the astronauts and ground crew had to follow. Capsule communicator Frank Gregg drew his chair towards his desk and leant forward towards the microphone.

"Apollo18, you are go for pyro arm and docking. We request you check and secure your cabin pressure."

"Copy that, control," said Wilson. "We're ready for C.S.M separation."

Commander Rossi's eyes scanned the control panel in front of him as he reached out and flicked four small switches into their start-up mode.

"Okay Andy, S.M R.C.S insole valves are all grey."

"Right, Dave, here we go."

Wilson pressed the pyro igniter switch, and instantly Titan thrust forward. Simultaneously the tapered cowling surrounding the lunar module began to open, its four segments folding backwards like the petals of a flower. Europer was now exposed and ready for docking. As Titan came to a stationary position, Wilson sat back in his seat and placed his hands around the two thruster control levers mounted either side of him. Gently twisting the right hand controller clockwise the R.C.S thruster's rockets, mounted in clusters of four round the circumference of the command module, burst into action. Slowly Titan began to revolve. Once again Wilson twisted the controller, applying another burst of thrust.

"Pitching at 2.5 degrees per second, Dave."

"Okay, you're looking good," replied the commander.

The three astronauts gazed through their windows, watching the stars moving from right to left in the blackness of space as Titan continued to negotiate its hundred and eighty degree turn. Slowly Europer came into view and Wilson reached out and lowered the target site which was mounted on a pivot above his window. This simple but important piece of equipment was a tube about six inches long with a one inch square piece of glass fixed to the end. A crosshair inside the glass would be lined up with a target site mounted on the side of the lunar module. Once the site and crosshair were in line, both space vehicles would be in the correct position for docking. Listening to the transmission back in the control room at Cape Kennedy, Saltzman and the rest of his team remained silent as the Apollo crew carried out their crucial manoeuvre. It was in the hands of Wilson to dock the two space vehicles correctly, or the mission would be aborted, and that would be a disaster for Saltzman who had waited years for this moment. As Wilson brought Titan in line with Europer, he gently pushed the left-hand control lever forward.

"Transition in forward motion," he said quietly, keeping his eye firmly on the crosshair and target site. The command module began to move sweetly and serenely towards Europa.

"Transition is looking good," said Stuart Martin as he watched the lunar module getting bigger in the capsule's windows, as the two space vehicles drew closer together.

Once again Wilson pushed the left hand control lever forward producing another burst of thrust. Slowly the probe mounted on the front of the capsule began to enter the docking adapter in the lunar module. Wilson glanced away from the target site to the control panel below. Then the command module gave a slight shudder as the two space vehicles locked together.

"Captured," said Wilson as a green contact light came on in front of him.

"Okay, let's retract," said Commander Rossi, flicking four switches simultaneously. The umbilical bolts holding the lunar module firmly in position detonated. Wilson pulled the left control lever towards him and the thrusters on the command module pulled both vehicles clear of the third stage of the Apollo rocket.

At Cape Kennedy Professor Steiner joined Saltzman. He turned and looked at the German rocket scientist and, after a moment's silence, he placed his hand on the Professor's shoulder.

"Gerhard, we've worked together for many years, let's not have disagreements now. We've waited a long time for this moment."

Steiner said nothing but nodded his head in agreement. Saltzman took a deep breath and shouted across the control room, "Well done gentlemen, next stop the Sinus Medii."

As the crew of Apollo 18 checked out the lunar module, Steve Curtis, back at the Baikanour Cosmodrome, had been brought to a security area. Zhurov had placed the American agent in a ten foot square room. In front of him was a small wooden table with two chairs. As he looked around he noticed there was no window or air ducting that he could escape through and interrogation, possibly by the KGB, was now certain. Then he heard footsteps on the concrete floor outside. Curtis came to the conclusion that there had to be at least three or four men heading his way. As he stared at the door, the footsteps came to a halt and he heard a key turn in the lock. The door was opened by a Russian soldier who then withdrew back into the corridor. A man in his late fifties then entered the room. He was about six foot two in height, weighed about two hundred and twenty pound, and wore a dark grey overcoat. With his white shirt, black trousers and pair of black, well-polished shoes, the man looked a forbidding character. He closed the door behind him and walked towards the table saying nothing. He sat down and glared straight into Curtis's eyes, and then he smiled.

"Mr Curtis," he said in a deep Ukrainian voice. "First may I thank you for returning the Mig 23 that you stole from us three years ago. We're curious to know why you've suddenly decided to return it to us."

Curtis looked straight at the Russian and said sarcastically, "Well, we decided that your aircraft was about ten years out of date so we thought we'd let you have it back. Do I get to know your name, seeing that you know mine?"

"Forgive me, Mr Curtis, my name is Major Yuri Laveikin of the KGB, and I would like you to know that there is a high price for stealing Russian aircraft."

Curtis nodded his head.

"Yes I have no doubt, but let's face it Major, both sides have stolen one another's technology since the end of the last war."

"Indeed we have, Mr Curtis, but you know that when you get caught you have to remain a prisoner just as our people are prisoners in your country are they not?"

Laveikin, sitting with his hands clasped together, leaned forward across the table. "There isn't much we don't know about you, Mr Curtis. Stephen James Curtis, born on the 11th of June 1927 in Denver, Colorado. Learnt to fly at the age of ten, flew solo from California to New York at the age of fourteen, and joined the USA air force at the age of twenty. I understand you were a top fighter pilot in the Korean War. Is that right, Mr Curtis?" asked the K.G.B officer smirking at the American. "On leaving the air force you joined the C.I.A in 1956. You quickly became one of their top agents and have accomplished many missions, notably against the U.S.S.R."

There was a moment's silence as the Russian continued to glare and grin at Curtis.

"You see, we know almost everything about you."

Curtis in his cheeky way replied, "Does it say in your dossier that I love bacon and eggs? I'm starving." Laveikin wasn't amused at Curtis's juvenile quip.

"You know it can be very cold in Siberia at this time of the year. It's a place they never get the chance to taste bacon and eggs. Now, for the last time, why are you here?"

Curtis remained silent. The American agent thought that if he kept quiet, Laveikin might slip up and reveal some information that could be of some use.

"We know you're not here to steal another aircraft that is for sure, and we also know that you have a secret Apollo mission heading towards the moon as we speak, do you not?"

Once again there was a moment of silence before Curtis spoke.

"Yes, you're right Major, we have a secret mission taking place at this very moment, although I don't think secret is a very good word to use seeing that you know all about it. Maybe you could tell me where you got your information from?"

Laveikin leaned back in his chair and laughed. "Mr Curtis, you have Russian rebels working for you, and so we have American renegades working for us."

Then there was another moment's silence as the two men looked at each other. The smile left Laveikin's face.

"You know, I often wonder who the real enemies are. Is it the likes of you and me, Mr Curtis? Patriots to our countries who are sent to fight each other, or is it the traitors who live amongst us? It's because of these people that you know all about us and we know all about you. Doesn't it make you feel angry when your own people sell you out, Mr Curtis?"

The American agent shrugged his shoulders and said, "That's the way it's always been Major. Even Christ himself had a traitor amongst his group, eager to sell him out. I guess there's something about the human race that will never change. As long as there's someone willing to pay the right price, there's always someone ready to accept it."

Laveikin pushed his chair back, stood up and began to walk across the small room. He turned and faced Curtis and leaned back against the wall.

"What price are you willing to pay for your life, Mr Curtis?"

The C.I.A agent just turned his head and looked at the Russian and said, "I'm not for sale, Major."

Laveikin folded his arms and smiled at Curtis. "We know your latest Apollo crew has been sent to investigate the glass structure on the moon."

"Glass structure, what are you talking about?" replied Curtis.

He decided to try bluffing in another attempt to prise more information from Laveikin.

"Don't play games with me, Mr Curtis," Laveikin shouted, as he walked back to the table. "The glass structure located at Sinus Medii, which was discovered ten years ago by the Soviet Union."

"Well, I'm afraid you've got the better of me Major because I know nothing about any glass structure," said Curtis, testing how far he could push the Russian.

"You're lying, and your country will not be allowed to succeed in removing the alien contents inside."

Still, Curtis tried to dig for more information, "If what you're saying is true, about this alien structure, I'm afraid to tell you that our Apollo spacecraft would have blasted off by now, which gives us a head start, wouldn't you say?"

"You're right, Mr Curtis," said Laveikin. "But what we have is a rocket which is more powerful than the Saturn 5. We will reach the moon before the American crew have had a chance to land."

Curtis paused for a moment. "You're going to blow the dome up, aren't you?"

"Correct," said Laveikin, smiling. "You see, you do know about this object, don't you, Mr Curtis. We believe a large bomb in the nosecone of our rocket should obliterate the alien structure completely, wouldn't you say?"

Curtis said nothing. Now that he knew what the Russians were planning, he realised he had to destroy the rocket or the Apollo crew would be killed if they got too close.

"Guards," shouted Laveikin.

Immediately the door opened and two Russian soldiers walked in.

"Take this man and dispose of him. You came here to destroy our rocket, Mr Curtis, and you have failed."

Laveikin moved away from the table. "Take him away," he said in a menacing voice.

Curtis stood up and, looking at one of the two soldiers, a great sense of relief came over him. The soldier was a little older, his skin dryer, but it didn't matter. The man dressed in the Russian uniform was his dear friend Sergei Tarelkin. Somehow the Russian had managed to enter the base undetected and join the group assigned to arrest Curtis. The American walked around the table and towards the two soldiers saying nothing. As he walked past them, Tarelkin and the second guard turned and began to walk either side of Curtis. The three men headed down the poorly lit corridor. Curtis glanced at Tarelkin hoping for some reaction, but the Russian looked straight ahead without acknowledging his old friend. As the three men reached the outer door of the building a military jeep stood at the main entrance. The driver of the vehicle started the engine, and Tarelkin climbed into the passenger seat next to him. The second guard pushed Curtis into the back seat so that the American sat diagonally opposite Tarelkin. Climbing into the jeep next to Curtis the guard shouted to the driver, "Detention block. Now."

The jeep quickly accelerated away from the interrogation unit and was soon out of sight. As they drove along the dimly lit road towards the detention centre, Curtis checked his watch. It was now 4:15am. Soon the sun would begin to rise over the base. He looked across at Tarelkin and, in the reflection in the window, he noticed the Russian gesture to him. He nodded to Curtis signalling to him to take out the guard. The American knew from past experiences of working with Tarelkin what the Russian had in mind. Curtis looked around him. In the darkness he could just make out the lights in the nearest building about half a mile away, and between them just open desolate ground. He glanced back at Tarelkin to give the all clear. Immediately the Russian drew back his arm, and with a tremendous blow slammed his elbow straight into the driver's temple. Curtis lunged at the guard next to him. With his left hand gripped tightly round the throat of the guard, the American rammed his right fist into the Russian's forehead. The guard, being pinned between the back seat and the full weight of Curtis's body, had very little chance to fight back, as the American slammed another right fist into his jaw. Tarelkin, with his right hand gripping the back of the driver's collar, thrust the semiconscious man's head hard into the steering wheel. The jeep was now out of control, veering left and right across the road. Tarelkin grabbed the driver by the chest and hurled him out of the vehicle. The man had very little chance of survival as his head hit the ground and the jeep's rear wheels crushed his legs.

Tarelkin leaped into the driver's seat and took control of the vehicle. He stamped hard on the brake pedal bringing the jeep to a sudden halt, which threw the second guard clean over the front passenger seat, slamming his head into the dashboard and breaking his neck instantly. Both men sat motionless for a moment as each regained his breath. Then, turning slightly and glancing over his shoulder,

Tarelkin looked at Curtis and said sarcastically, "It's good to see you again, some things never change for us do they?"

chapter six
WIN OR LOSE

"How the hell have you managed to get into the base?" asked Curtis.

"I've been acting as a security guard for the last week, thanks to my contacts working here," said Tarelkin. "No more questions Curtis, we don't have much time. The rocket is almost ready for launching, but first we must dispose of these two."

Putting the jeep into reverse, Tarelkin drove back along the road to where the driver lay. Stopping the jeep he jumped out, ran towards the dead man and knelt down beside him. Lifting the driver over his shoulder he turned to Curtis.

"Quickly. Bring the other one."

Curtis leapt out the back of the jeep. Pulling the second guard across his shoulder and lifting him out of the vehicle, he headed for the side of the road where Tarelkin had dumped the driver into a ditch.

"Put him here, then remove his jacket and put it on."

Curtis lowered the man to the ground and removed his jacket. Tarelkin ran back to the jeep, started it up and turned it one hundred and eighty degrees. Curtis jumped into the front seat next to the Russian and they sped off towards the launch area.

"Sergei, the Russians are going to destroy the dome before we reach the moon. I have to stop that rocket, but first you have to take me to the fuel processing area."

"What are you planning to do?"

"I'm going to blow that rocket up before it takes off."

Tarelkin checked his watch. "I'm afraid we're running out of time. There is only thirty minutes before the launch, and it's too late for any sabotage attempt."

"Trust me," said Curtis. "We won't have to touch the rocket."

"Trust you? I must be mad," laughed Tarelkin as he manoeuvred the jeep around the winding road which led to the fuel storage area.

"Do you know anything about this new engine your rocket engineers have developed?" asked Curtis.

"Its uses what they call a nuclear pulse," said Tarelkin. "Once out in space the engine produces a tiny nuclear explosion that propels the spacecraft at an incredible speed. It will reach the moon in hours rather than days."

"My God, we'd better move fast," said Curtis.

As Tarelkin drove towards the processing plant, Curtis sat quietly thinking. He found it hard to believe that the Russians were about to destroy the most important artefact the human race had ever discovered. Out of pure selfishness the two superpowers of the planet earth would rather obliterate the alien structure than share its contents. How could mankind learn about the universe if every time he discovered something, he would act in such a shameful way.

"The plant is just around this bend," said Tarelkin as he began to slow down. As they approached the security gate, Curtis looked up towards the floodlights illuminating the entire area.

"The plant's too well lit Sergei, we're going to be seen by everyone."

"Of course we are. The more we do in front of our enemies' noses the more likely they are to ignore us."

As the jeep approached the checkpoint the security barrier was raised. Curtis couldn't believe the extreme ease in which he and Tarelkin were allowed to enter the area without anyone checking their identity.

"See what I mean," said Tarelkin turning and smiling at the American. A large dome at least fifty feet high and one hundred feet at the base stood to the left hand side of the road.

"This is the main fuel processing plant," said Tarelkin. "What are you planning to do?"

"I'll show you," replied Curtis as he noticed a large fuel tanker parked alongside the plant. "Pull alongside that tanker."

Tarelkin drove towards the sixty foot long vehicle and stopped alongside the cab.

"Wait here," said Curtis climbing out of the jeep.

"Steve, we only have twenty minutes before the rocket is launched. Whatever you're thinking of doing, you had better do it now."

"Right," said Curtis as he ran around the front of the cab to the driver's side. Climbing upwards and opening the door he looked at the driver, smiled and said, "Dobroye utro," meaning, 'good morning.'

"Dobroye utro," replied the driver. Curtis lifted himself a little higher up towards the Russian and immediately he rammed his right fist into the man's jaw, knocking him out cold. He then leaned backwards looking left and right, checking that there were no other personnel in the facility. Opening the door and grabbing the driver by the lapels of his uniform, Curtis dragged the unconscious Russian out of the cab and sent him hurtling to the ground. Tarelkin came running to the side of the vehicle as the American agent leapt down beside him.

"What are you doing?"

"I haven't got time to explain Sergei. Get rid of him while I check this tanker."

Tarelkin dragged the driver to the side of the processing building hoping his body wouldn't be discovered too soon. Curtis ran to the rear of the tanker and placed his hands against the side of the vehicle. He could feel the freezing cold temperature of the liquid oxygen inside. A six inch valve at the base of the tanker had a thin layer of ice around the outlet pipe and Curtis realised that the vehicle was full of the volatile liquid. He ran back towards the cab where Tarelkin was waiting.

"Quick, get in the jeep and take me to the launch pad."

Without questioning the American, Tarelkin ran to the jeep while Curtis climbed into the tanker. Both men started the engines of their vehicles. Tarelkin turned the jeep around and headed back to the road, while Curtis quickly put the tanker into gear. Slowly the vehicle began to roll forward as the American eased out the clutch. Tarelkin realised they were running out of time, but drove slowly towards the checkpoint. The last thing he and Curtis needed was to be stopped and questioned. As they approached the barrier one of the two guards walked towards the edge of the road and raised his hand.

"Damn," thought Tarelkin. "Not now."

He brought the jeep to a halt, with Curtis stopping the tanker only a few feet behind. Keeping ice cool the Russian gently smiled at the guard as he approached.

"Identification," said the guard.

Tarelkin didn't waste a second. He immediately drew from his inside pocket a forged identity card, which had been passed on to him by his contact at the base. Shining a torch onto the I.D, then onto Tarelkin's face, the officer raised his hand to give the all clear to open the check point.

"Come on, come on," thought Curtis. "We're running out of time."

The security gate slid gently open and Curtis gave a sigh of relief as he realised that he and

Tarelkin weren't going to be questioned. Both vehicles began to pull away from the checkpoint. Curtis glanced at his watch.

"Fifteen minutes to launch," he thought to himself, "and we're six miles away from the launch pad."

He glanced across to the east side of the rocket base. A slight tinge of dark blue began to edge its way onto the horizon.

"Soon be daybreak. We've got to get to that rocket," he thought as they sped towards the launch site.

In the launch centre, flight controller Vladimir Manarov looked across at his flight technicians. Each man was checking the technical data on the monitors in front of him. As he watched he was joined by a Russian army general, Uri Aksyonov.

"Soon Vladimir, we will be on our way, will we not? With the new fuel and engine powering our rocket, we will reach the moon before the Americans and destroy the prize they have worked so hard to obtain."

Manarov wasn't so optimistic. He had seen the new engine explode three times during testing, while a whole team of engineers had died from inhaling the poisonous gases given off by the new fuel. He just looked at Aksyonov and said quietly, "Yes General."

Now only three miles from the launch pad Tarelkin and Curtis could see the rocket standing upright. Its four umbilical arms were holding the vehicle rigidly in position over the flame trench which would deflect the rockets exhaust away from the launch tower. Tarelkin stopped the jeep, forcing Curtis to stop behind him. Climbing out of his vehicle the Russian ran to the side of the tanker and looked up at the American.

"Okay, now what."

Curtis leaned out of the driver's window and shouted down to Tarelkin, "Sergei I need you to get me to the entrance of the flame trench, and then I want you to follow me."

"Right," replied the Russian as he ran back to the jeep.

He began to realize what Curtis was planning, and with only minutes to lift off, he knew both of them would be cutting things pretty fine. The two men set off once again towards the launch tower. Tarelkin then swerved off the road and steered the jeep across the uneven terrain.

Curtis followed, the tanker rocking from side to side as it struck small stones and the undulations of the land. Then he saw the entrance to the flame trench. As Tarelkin steered the jeep to one side, Curtis drove past him, driving the tanker as fast as he could along the narrow concrete trench towards the launch pad. Curtis looked out at the twenty foot high concrete walls either side of him, taking care to keep the tanker in the centre of the trench.

"I mustn't hit these walls," he thought to himself, as he kept his foot hard down on the gas pedal. Speed was essential but if the tanker hit the walls he could rip the vehicle open spraying liquid oxygen in all directions.

In the control room the final countdown had begun. Tee minus thirty seconds and counting.

Now with only fifty yards to the launch pad, Curtis looked up at the Russian rocket towering in front of him, with the sky getting brighter as the sun began to rise over the base. He drove the tanker directly beneath the spaceship then hit the brakes hard causing the vehicle to slide slightly from side to side. Stopping the tanker beneath the rocket's engines, he leaped from the cab and ran to the rear of the long vehicle faster than he'd ever run in his life.

Tarelkin had kept the jeep within yards of the tanker as he'd followed Curtis along the flame trench so the American would have time to escape.

He leapt into the passenger seat, and turned to the Russian.

"Let's get the hell out of here," he shouted.

Having no time or space to turn the jeep around, Tarelkin slammed the jeep into reverse gear, and within seconds they were heading backwards along the flame trench.

"Fifteen seconds and counting," called out the launch controller, as the Russian technicians waited anxiously for the engines to ignite." Fourteen, thirteen, twelve," the countdown continued.

Tarelkin, his foot hard on the gas pedal, fought desperately to keep the jeep straight as it sped along the narrow trench.

"Ten, nine, eight, ignition sequence start."

The engines in the central core of the rocket ignited. One second later the four tapered booster rockets simultaneously burst into life. As the thrust built up, the flame bore down onto the tanker below and cut through the metal like a giant blow torch.

Instantly the whole vehicle exploded sending metal and pieces of concrete from the flame trench upwards. The debris slammed into the rocket at high velocity tearing fuel lines and puncturing the shell of the boosters. Fuel began to rain down into the inferno below instantly catching fire. The ignited fuel began to run back into the rocket's main fuel tanks and with a mighty explosion the space vehicle, launch pad, umbilical arms, and the surrounding area was engulfed in an enormous fireball. With flames rushing towards them, Tarelkin kept his foot hard on the gas. Wrestling with the steering wheel, the Russian found it hard to stop the sides of the jeep from scraping the concrete walls, but it was this or burn to death. The two men had no option but to keep going. As the launch pad continued to disintegrate, the tiny jeep's rear wheels struck a small boulder, sending the vehicle bouncing three feet into the air.

"Ease down, Sergei. Come on ease down we're clear," shouted Curtis.

The Russian eased off the gas pedal bringing the vehicle to a halt. Both men sat back in their seats, both of them gasping for air and looking at the carnage ahead of them. There were still small explosions erupting from the flames as small amounts of fuel ignited.

"What now?" asked Tarelkin.

"We've got to get out of here," replied Curtis. "I need to get back to the airfield. Can you get me there?"

"For sure, but the place will be swarming with people. How are you going to get out?"

"I'm going to steal another Mig 23."

Tarelkin looked at the American in disbelief. "I don't know how you have the nerve."

"Nerve?" replied Curtis. "That's the one thing you have to have plenty of in this job."

Tarelkin engaged first gear on the jeep and soon had the vehicle racing towards the airfield eight miles east of their present position. As they drove away from the launch area, which was still a raging fireball, Russian firefighting and army vehicles headed towards them.

"Get down," said Tarelkin as he pushed Curtis below the dashboard. "Don't let them see you," he shouted.

The vehicles approached at high speed. Tarelkin, still wearing his Russian uniform, raised his right arm and acknowledged the oncoming convoy. The fire fighters at the front of the line signaled back, without even bothering to stop and check out the Russian. They were more concerned about reaching the fire than asking questions. They were followed by four large army trucks filled with some of the rocket base's personnel, though it would be too late for any of them to do anything, as the launch area was completely destroyed.

Curtis sat up in is seat. "You say I've got a nerve!"

Tarelkin smiled. "What was that you said to me? That's the one thing you need plenty of in this job?"

As they approached the airfield, Curtis crouched low in his seat once more.

"Sergei, drive round to the right hand side of the hangar then I'll jump out."

Tarelkin drove carefully round the side on the building looking in all directions for any personnel who might notice them. Bringing the jeep to a halt, Tarelkin checked again.

There were vehicles dashing around in all directions. The activity around the base was on high alert. It seemed everyone on duty was being called upon for assistance.

"Okay, you're clear," said Tarelkin.

Curtis sat up and looked around. "Right, I'd better get going." He looked at the Russian and shook his hand. "Thanks again, Sergei. Are you going to be alright?"

"Sure," said the Russian. "I'll get out the same way I got in, through the front gate. Wearing this uniform no-one will ask too many questions. Now get going and good luck."

Curtis leapt from the jeep and headed towards the hangar doorway as Tarelkin sped away in the jeep, heading for the main entrance of the base. Neither man knew whether they would see each other again, or if either would escape, but they were professionals and each one appreciated the dangers and risks of their missions. There was no time to think of each other now, it was each man for himself, and Curtis was in trouble. They knew the American's face so it was important to keep low and not be noticed. He ran along the edge of the hangar towards the entrance. Pressing his body against the wall he carefully peered inside. The hangar was at least a hundred feet in length, and Curtis could see four air frame technicians busily working on a large transport plane at the far end of the building. Standing outside on the tarmac stood the three Mig 23's. The one he had arrived in, and the other two which had been fully fuelled and armed by the Russian ground crew. Curtis carefully stepped into the hangar and looked around. Sensing it was safe to move, he crept carefully into the building, keeping his body close to the wall and looking for objects that he could use to hide behind if the circumstances required it. He moved along the hangar looking for the pilots' suiting up room. Suddenly, several yards in front of him, a door opened. He quickly dived towards a crate containing aircraft parts and crouched behind it. Two men emerged from the room, ran across the hangar towards the transport plane and began to shout orders at the men working on the aircraft. There was still a lot of excitement on the base following the catastrophic failure of the launch of the rocket. Curtis thought that while the base personnel had their minds on the rocket disaster, he could make his move. Emerging from behind a crate he quickly ran to the room where the two Russians had been working. He slowly opened the door and quietly walked inside. On the far side of the room was another door, which led to the pilots changing area. Without a moment's delay he slipped into the room, closing the door behind him.

"Thank heaven," he thought.

In the right hand corner stood a small rack, about six feet in length, and hanging neatly from it were four flight suits. Curtis crossed the room and took one of the helmets, carefully placing it over his head. In the hangar, Russian air force Major, Anatoli Gorbatko had rounded up the technicians inside the building. The eight men stood in a semicircle around him as the Major began to address them.

"Three hours ago, an American secret service agent infiltrated our base. We have reason to believe that he is responsible for sabotaging our rocket. I want this man caught, and I want him alive."

Gorbatko pointed to the four men to his left. "I want you men to search the perimeter of the airfield. The rest of you are to bring in the three Migs from outside and then I want you to seal this hangar. This American is capable of flying our aircraft, and there's a good chance he may try to make his escape in one of them. Do it now."

The eight men quickly dispersed to follow Gorbatko's orders. Out of the four technicians detailed to the Migs, one of them, Yuri Levchenko, ran to a maintenance haulage truck located near the entrance of the hangar. This vehicle was used by the ground crew to manoeuvre the Migs around the airfield when maintenance to the aircraft was required. The other three ran outside towards the aircraft which had been fully serviced and ready for use.

"We'll take this one into the hangar first then return for the other," said one of them.

The Russian ground crew watched as Levchenko drove the truck from the hangar and lined it up the with the nose wheel of the Mig. As the connecting arm which was attached to the front of the vehicle drew within twelve inches of the front undercarriage, the three men lifted it off the ground and connected the arm to a pivot mounted two feet above the nose wheel.

Levchenko steadily let out the clutch of the maintenance truck and began to push the Mig backwards. Slowly the aircraft was manoeuvred over the tarmac until inch by inch it entered the hangar. With the Russian ground crews concentration firmly on manoeuvring the Mig, neither of them noticed the door of the suiting-up room open. Standing in the doorway and dressed in a Russian pilot's flight suit was Curtis. As the technicians disconnected the connecting arm from the Mig's nose wheel, Levchenko engaged reverse gear on the maintenance truck and reversed the vehicle in the direction of the second aircraft standing outside. The rest of the ground crew followed leaving the first Mig unguarded. Curtis realised it was now or never. He sprinted across the hangar towards the Russian fighter plane. Leaping onto the trailing edge of the starboard wing he ran towards the fuselage. Jumping onto the centre section of the aircraft, he headed towards the cockpit. Carefully he climbed round the open glass canopy, lowered himself into the pilot's seat and began to power up the aircraft's electrical systems. The air intake fans on the Khachaturov R-35-300 turbojet began to rotate. Within a few moments the jet's engines began to roar, the thrust building by the second. Immediately the Russian ground crew, still connecting the maintenance truck to the other aircraft, stopped and turned towards the hangar entrance. Curtis now had the

Mig rolling and with one of its missiles locked onto the second fighter, he pressed the release button. With a whoosh of tail fire, the interceptor shot toward its target. The second Mig exploded into an enormous fireball, the blast sending debris and ground crew in all directions. Lifting the visor on his helmet, Curtis looked out of the cockpit canopy for any other airfield personnel. He steered his Mig around the inferno and headed towards the runway, the GSH -23L twin barrel gun ready if needed. He could see the fire burning five miles away at the launch site, the Russians desperately continuing to bring it under control. As the runway lights came into view, Curtis turned the aircraft and lined it up on the centre line. Opening the throttle, of the aircraft, the G- forces pushed Curtis back into his seat as the Mig began to race down the runway. Within a few moments the Russian fighter plane reached its take-off speed and Curtis eased the control column towards himself. The nose of the Mig rose effortlessly as its pilot reached down to his right and pulled back on the lever to retract the undercarriage. Levelleing out the aircraft, and flying as low as possible to avoid being detected by enemy radar, Curtis knew the Russians would stop at nothing to try and shoot him down. His eyes scanned across the instrument panel. Keeping an eye on his compass the American agent began to punch the co-ordinates into the on-board computer which would direct the Mig towards Turkey. Slowly the aircraft began to bank to the left while simultaneously the compass rotated until the instrument was reading west.

"Good, we're on the correct course," he thought. "Now it's up to Rossi and the Apollo crew."

The American began to relax as he realized the Baikanour rocket base was well behind him. With his mission accomplished and the R7 rocket destroyed, it was now up to the Apollo crew to bring the secrets of the alien dome back to earth for the western world to examine. Curtis wondered how Saltzman and Majestic would use the alien technology.

"It certainly won't be for the good of mankind that's for sure," he thought. "Contact with an alien race will be the last thing the people of the world will learn about. Whatever is in that dome will be for Saltzman and his shareholders to profiteer from."

Curtis couldn't help being cynical. He'd seen this sort of thing too many times as a C.I.A agent - laying his life on the line for a so called good cause, only to see the selfish attitudes of a few take everything that could benefit so many. Checking the instrument panel again, and making a slight course correction, Curtis kept the Mig on its westerly trajectory knowing that the Turkish base was only a few hours away.

Three days later, the crew of Apollo 18 was in orbit around the moon. Sixty nautical miles above the lunar surface, Rossi, Martin and Wilson were preparing the two space vehicles, Titan and Europa, for separation. As the two spaceships emerged from the far side of the moon, command module pilot Wilson attempted to make contact with the control centre at Cape Kennedy.

"Titan to central control, Titan to central control, do you read? Over," said Wilson.

Back on earth Saltzman, Professor Steiner and their technical personnel sat anxiously waiting.

"This is cap com to eighteen, reading you loud and clear Andy," said capsule communicator Frank Gregg.

"Roger," replied Wilson. "Europa separation in tee minus five minutes."

Saltzman and the professor stood at the back of the control room listening carefully to the transmission from Apollo. Saltzman, rubbing his hands with excitement, turned to Steiner.

"It will only be a couple of hours now professor, and it's all ours."

The professor knew that as soon as Europa landed, radio contact with the three astronauts would be shut down. A pre-recorded fictitious mission would be transmitted from the lunar module, to deceive the world into believing that the mission was about trying to find a rare mineral.

In the lunar module Rossi and Martin made final instrument checks before the separation.

"Stuart, I think we'd better check the high-gain antenna," said Rossi. "We want to send a good audio transmission back to earth before we land. Make sure the sequence camera is disconnected too, the last thing we want is to transmit pictures."

"Okay, Dave, will do," replied Martin.

Andrew Wilson gazed across the instrument panel of the command module.

"Tee minus one minute and counting for separation."

"Okay Andy," replied Rossi.

Back in the control centre at Cape Kennedy, all personnel waited nervously for the descent of Europa. Frank Gregg took one final sip of his coffee and then prepared himself to receive and relay instructions to the lunar module. Wilson broke the silence as he sat totally alone at the controls of the command module.

"Separation five seconds, four, three, two, one, zero."

The thrusters on Europa ignited, pushing the space vehicles apart. Wilson watched though the windows of his command ship as the spidery looking lunar module began to pull away.

"How are we looking, Stu?" asked Rossi.

"Okay. We'll go for power descent at forty six thousand feet."

"Roger that."

At this point the lunar module was lying in a horizontal position with its window facing the moon's surface. This gave Rossi and Martin a brief moment to look out and observe the bleak terrain below them before they began their power descent.

In the control room Frank Gregg tried to keep contact with the lunar module. Briefly losing the radio signal between himself and the spacecraft he immediately reported the situation to the crew.

"Europa, this is control, do you read? Over."

There was a moment's pause before Gregg repeated his transmission.

"Europa, this is control, do you read? Over."

Once again there was a short pause before Martin replied.

"Roger control, reading you loud and clear. I believe there could be some oscillation in the high gain antenna Frank," said Martin. "I'll try adjusting it again when we turn the spacecraft around."

"Copy that, Stuart," said Gregg, his eyes glued to the control panel in front of him, as he continued to relay instructions to the two astronauts.

Europa, we recommend you yaw nine degrees to the right.

This may strengthen the high gain signal."

"Roger control," replied Martin.

Rossi listened to the transmissions between his co-pilot and earth as he wrapped his right hand around the thrust control lever. Carefully twisting it to the right, the yaw thrusters jerked the lunar module clockwise placing the high gain antenna in a better position for transmitting.

"Okay Europa, we're getting a better signal now," said Gregg.

"Roger Frank," said Martin as he checked the instrument panel again. "I've got the residuals on the abort guidance system, for your control. They are minus 0.1, minus 0.2, and minus 0.7." As the residual figures echoed around the control room, guidance technician Tony Williamson checked Martin's figures on his computer.

"Okay, Frank, Stuart's good here," said Williamson with a loud confident voice.

"Europa, you're looking great. You are ready for power descent."

"Roger control."

Martin turned to his right and began to flick several switches mounted on a small control panel above him.

"Okay, Dave, stabilisation and control circuit breakers on. D.E.C.A gimbals on. AC closed, and command override off. Gimbals enabled, and rate scale twenty five."

"Roger, Stuart," replied Rossi. "We're go on the AGS alignment, on my mark 1.20 for ignition."

Rossi flicked the guidance switches on the control panel above him as Martin began to read down the lunar module's landing procedure checklist.

"Thrust translation for jets. Balance coupler on TCA. Throttle to minimum auto C.O.R."

"What's the A.G.S reading?" interrupted Rossi.

"It's reading four hundred plus. Standing by for engaging engine arm for descent."

"Roger that," replied Rossi.

As the lunar module continued its descent, Martin took another glance through the window. The lunar surface, now getting closer by the minute, began to reveal amazing detail. As a geologist Martin was amazed at the magnificent craters and mountains untouched since time began. He wondered what the alien race that built the glass dome might have thought as they approached the moon for the first time.

Did they look upon it with the same astonishment as Martin did, or was space travel so common to the aliens that landing on another world was just a routine operation? Suddenly Gregg's voice came over the radio.

"Europa, we request you pitch your spacecraft two hundred and twelve degrees and yaw thirty seven, over."

"Roger, will do. Just finishing landmark tracking before we pitch Frank." replied Martin.

Landmark tracking required the two astronauts to confirm their trajectory before pitching the lunar module in its vertical position. Peering through the windows, the two astronauts looked carefully for the crater known as Ukert. Once this crater was spotted they knew their landing site would be just twenty five miles down range of their present position. Now things were getting tense as the tiny spacecraft began to fly over the Sinus Medii. Suddenly Rossi called out, "Stuart, look down there."

The commander pointed to the left hand side of his window. There, fifty thousand feet below them, was Ukert.

"Control, have target crater in sight, beginning to pitch."

In the control room Gregg, Saltzman, Steiner and the rest of the technical team, looked up at the T.V screen mounted on the control room wall in front of them. They could see the icon representing the lunar module moving from right to left as Europa descended to the moon's surface. Commander Rossi took his eyes off the lunar surface and began to check the instruments on the control panel.

"We'd better keep a constant check on the high gain antenna, Stuart. We don't want to lose contact with earth at a crucial moment."

"Roger, Dave. I'll keep an eye on it."

The lunar module continued its descent, with everything looking good for the two astronauts, as they approached the lunar surface.

"Engine armed, descent forty seconds," said Martin, continuing to give Rossi instructions.

"Okay, Stu, override five seconds. Descent armed. Switch on altitude light."

"Roger, altitude light on."

Rossi scanned his eyes across the control panel. Happy with the altitude of the spacecraft and with the systems on board looking good, the commander gave the order, "Okay, Stu, go for power descent, ignition."

"Roger ignition."

Martin pressed the ignition button, and instantly the descent engine ignited with a tremendous roar.

"We have ignition," called the lunar module pilot. "Throttle at ten percent."

Back in the control room the technical team's eyes were glued to the large monitor in front of them. They watched as the icon representing the lunar module began to move slowly across the screen as the descent engine reduced the speed of the space vehicle. The burn time at ten percent would last for twenty six seconds as the lunar module's computer calculated the ignition time for the main throttle up.

"Rate of descent is looking good, Dave," said Martin calmly, as Europa continued to fall towards the moon. At his desk in the control room Gregg checked the data coming in on his computer.

"Europa, this is control. S-band pitch is minus nine, yaw plus eighteen."

"Roger," replied Rossi. "Stu, I'm getting a little fluctuation in the A.C voltage."

"Okay, Dave. It's probably just the meter, so don't worry we're still looking good at three minutes. Rate of descent is good and the altitude is right on."

Rossi, his hands gently pitching and rolling the spacecraft into position took a quick glance out of his window. The land scape looked familiar thanks to the photographs that the commander had studied days before take-off from earth. "Stuart, from the look of some of these landmarks we're not going to be far away from our target."

"Great," said Martin. "We're still looking good at four minutes. Continue power descent."

"Right, lock on the landing radar."

"Roger will do."

Martin immediately carried out his commander's order and within seconds a radar signal emitted from Europa bounced back from the lunar surface to the spacecraft, giving an altitude reading.

"Altitude thirty three thousand feet, Dave."

Rossi, concentrating hard on his task of landing Europa, glanced once again out of the spacecraft's window. Checking for familiar landmarks the commander's heart beat increased slightly, till Martin's reassuring voice called out, "Still looking good, Dave, rate of descent is good."

Rossi took a quick glance at the controls. Concerned about the fuel supply he asked Martin for a status check.

"How are we looking on the Delta-H, Stu?"

"Delta-H is good, altitude now thirty three thousand feet.

Control we're now six minutes twenty five seconds into the burn."

"Roger Europa," said Gregg. "We request you throttle down, Dave."

"Roger that," replied the Commander, as he began to decelerate the space vehicle.

"Are we still looking good on the Delta-H?"

"Yes, it's coming down beautifully, no problem."

Europa continued its descent to the lunar surface. Martin still kept a check on the landmarks as detail in craters and valleys became more prominent.

Watching the larger monitor in front of them, Gregg and the technical team noticed the radio signal from the spacecraft began to falter.

"Europa, this is control, we're losing your signal on the high gain antenna again."

"Roger control," said Martin as he glanced at Rossi. "I'm going to take the antenna out of slow mode and switch to auto, Dave, that way the computer will keep the antenna pointing towards Earth regardless of our altitude."

"Okay, Stu."

Outside the spacecraft the high gain antenna began to pitch and roll into position as Martin switched it to automatic. Sending its signal across the void of space directly to the control room at Cape Kennedy, contact with Europa was quickly resumed. The icon on the large screen and the data on the technician's computers showed the lunar module to be on course and descending on its correct trajectory.

"She's looking good, isn't she Professor?" said Saltzman to the German rocket scientist.

"Yes, she is. I wonder how long it will be before they have visual contact."

"I don't know," said the industrialist. "But when they do I hope to God they keep their mouths shut. Other radars around the world could be listening in."

Back on the spacecraft the two astronauts concentrated harder than ever as the lunar module reached its correct altitude.

"Coming up to eight minutes, Dave," said Martin. "Control, can you give us an estimated pitch over time please?"

"Roger Europa," said Gregg. "The computer has now initiated approach phase program P-64. Your altitude is five thousand feet, rate of descent one hundred feet per second."

The lunar surface was approaching fast. Rossi and Martin knew the dome couldn't be far away now. Their spacecraft was well in the target area and Rossi was anxious to pitch Europa into its vertical position.

"Control, I'm going to manual. Preparing to pitch."

"Copy that," said Gregg. "You're looking good, coming up on nine minutes."

Rossi looked across at Martin.

"Okay, Stu, here we go. Keep a look out for it," he said quietly.

"Roger, Dave."

"Right P.G.N.S mode, switch to altitude hold."

Rossi switched the mode controller from auto to manual; then he gently wrapped his fingers around the hand controller once more. He slowly eased it forward and instantly a burst of gas from the pitch thrusters began to tilt the lunar module ninety degrees. For a brief moment the two astronauts' view of the lunar surface was lost as Europa pitched over. Then the two of them waited anxiously for the moon to reappear in their windows. As the lunar horizon came into view Martin's eyes opened wide at the sight before him. He turned towards Rossi. Without saying a word he took his commander's left arm, shook it gently and pointed towards the landscape ahead of them. Rossi looked away from the control panel for a moment and looked out of his window. There before them, standing one mile high at its centre and a mile and a half in diameter stood the glass dome. It was a magnificent sight. Even from that distance they could make out its intricate frame work which was covered in a beautiful green glass material. It could only be approximately eight to ten miles away, and Europa still had forward velocity as it was descending. The lunar module was closing in on its target every second, as Martin began to pat Rossi on the back to congratulate his Commander.

"Control this is Europa. We have the target landing site. I repeat we have the target landing site," said Rossi.

At Cape Kennedy control centre Saltzman clenched his fist and punched the air. He knew as soon as Rossi said those words that the dome was in sight. He walked briskly towards the front of the control room where Frank Gregg was sitting and patted the capsule communicator on the back.

"We copy you Europa, you are go for landing, repeat, go for landing."

"Roger," replied Rossi in a loud voice. "Three thousand feet at seventy, give me an L.P.D Stuart."

"Roger, will do."

By using the landing point designator the two astronauts could retarget the lunar module on its descent bringing them closer to the dome.

"Into the A.G.S. forty degrees," said Martin as Europa was now approximately five miles away.

"We're one thousand feet at thirty."

Rossi concentrated hard on controlling the lunar module manually while listening to Martin giving altitude readings.

"Altitude seven hundred and fifty, down at twenty three feet per second."

The descent engine was now at full throttle. Europa slowing down beautifully on its final approach. Martin, now too busy to look out of the window, had his eyes firmly fixed on the control panel in front of him.

There was no time to make a mistake now. Concentration was everything and giving Rossi the correct data was imperative.

"Altitude five hundred and fifty feet, down at fifteen feet per second."

There was a short pause and then Martin continued, "Altitude four hundred feet down at nine."

At the Kennedy space Centre everyone sat quietly. No one dared say a word for fear of breaking the concentration of the two astronauts. Saltzman, with both fists clenched, spoke quietly to himself, "Come on Rossi, land it, land it."

Europa was nearly there, its descent engine still burning at full throttle, as Martin continued to give his readings.

"Three hundred and fifty feet down at four."

"We're looking good, Stuart, keep readings coming," called Rossi.

"Okay. Two hundred feet, three and a half down. Nearly there, Dave. One hundred and fifty feet, six and a half down."

With his right hand still gently caressing the hand controller, Rossi thrust the lunar module to the right slightly.

"How's the fuel, Stuart?" he asked anxiously.

"Five percent remaining, Dave. We're looking good. Seventy five feet, down a half, six forward."

There was another moment of silence from the two astronauts as Europa's descent engine rapidly burned away what remained of the fuel.

"Thirty feet, two and half down. Thirty seconds of fuel remaining. Twenty feet, down half."

Europa was only moments away from touchdown. The dust from the lunar surface was being blown in all directions by the thrust of the descent engine, as Martin gave his final readings.

"Ten feet, half down. Five feet."

The four foot pads of the lunar module finally made contact with the lunar surface, the weight of the space vehicle pressing them hard into the grey powder like surface.

"Contact light," shouted Martin.

Rossi and Martin felt the craft shudder slightly as Europa gently came to rest on the lunar surface.

"Okay, Stuart, engine stop, ACA out of detent. Mode control both auto. Descent engine command override off. Engine arm off. Four, one, three circuit is in.

"Okay, Dave, congratulations," said a relieved Stuart Martin as he leaned over towards his Commander and shook him by the hand.

"We copy you down Europa," said Gregg. "Congratulations, you're now go to start the E.V.A."

Rossi and Martin knew at once that the words 'go to start mission' meant they were to shut down all radio transmissions and proceed totally alone. They weren't even to transmit to Wilson orbiting the moon in the command module. The only time contact with each other and Earth would be permissible, was when the two astronauts were ready to lift off from the Moon surface. Gregg, still seated at his desk in the control centre, turned to Saltzman.

"Well they're on their own now. There isn't anything we can do till they're ready to make contact."

"Have you got your script at hand, Mr Gregg?" asked Saltzman with smug satisfaction, as everything seemed to be going to plan.

"Sure." Gregg picked up an A4 size yellow folder from the left side of his desk and waved it at Saltzman.

"Excellent, Mr Gregg. Get on with it."

Saltzman walked briskly towards the exit door of the control room. "I'm going back to my room gentlemen. I want to know straight away when Rossi and Martin are ready to take off from the moon."

Inside the lunar module, the two astronauts had suited themselves up for their E.V.A. Their one hundred and eighty pound bulky Teflon fibre spacesuit would thankfully only weigh one sixth of its mass on the moon. Both men had worked for months getting familiar with the lunar gravity by training in a swimming pool size water tank back on earth. This was standard training for all Apollo astronauts, as moving around in deep water simulated the type of motion they would experience on the moon. Before Rossi opened the hatch of the lunar module, there was one important task to perform.

"Okay, Stuart, let's have the tape."

Martin opened up a plastic cassette box and removed a cassette with a recording on it which would last three hours. On the tape was the fake mission that both astronauts had pre-recorded at Area 51 three weeks before launch. It was well scripted by Saltzman and his team, and had been prepared with pauses perfectly timed, so Frank Gregg back at the control centre could answer. If anyone was listening back home, it would sound like a perfectly normal mission. Rossi placed the cassette into a small player fixed to the side of the main control panel. With the high gain antenna pointing directly to earth, the commander pressed the play button, and the bogus mission began to transmit.

"Okay control, we're about to start our E.V.A," said Rossi's recorded voice. "I would like to apologise to people back on Earth who were hoping to watch what we're doing up here, but we've lost the video signal on the antenna. I'm afraid to say that this mission is going to be sound only, so I hope you aren't losing any interest."

This was a fabrication of course. All the cameras on the two space vehicles had been disconnected just before the descent.

"Right, Stuart, the tape's rolling, let's get moving," said Rossi.

The two astronauts were equipped with short-range transmitters and receivers so they could be in contact with each other.

Rossi slowly opened the hatch of the spacecraft and looked out across the lunar surface. There ahead of him, only one mile away, stood the glass dome.

"Stuart, take a look at this," said the Commander with great excitement.

Martin crouched down alongside Rossi and looked out at the magnificent structure standing a mile high. They had managed to land the lunar module so close to the dome that they could see quite clearly hundreds of pentagon shaped tube sections linked to each other to form one huge assembly. This framework was covered in glass, which possessed a beautiful green tint. However, many of the glass sections were broken. It was obvious that, over the centuries, tiny particles of meteoric dust had slammed into the structure at many thousands of miles an hour. Although still a magnificent sight and masterful piece of engineering, it was clear to the two astronauts that the structure had been derelict for many centuries.

"Just look at that sucker, Dave," said the amazed Stuart Martin. "What kind of race could have built such a place?"

"A race that is far more advanced than us, that's for sure. Come on, let's deploy the lunar rover."

Rossi slowly inched himself feet first out of the spacecraft. The astronaut climbed down the ladder rung by rung, as if moving in slow motion. Martin watched until his commanding officer was halfway down the steps, then he, like Rossi, slowly inched himself out of Europa. Martin waited crouched down on top of the ladder till Rossi had made his giant leap for mankind before starting his descent. As Rossi's feet hit the moon surface, he watched the lunar dust slowly rise about six inches off the ground, before gradually returning to the surface.

"Amazing," he thought to himself as he turned and looked at the dome. "Can you hear me, Stu?"

"Yes, no problem," said the geologist as he stepped onto the lunar surface.

"Let's get the Rover, we don't have much time."

Normal walking was impossible on the moon in the one sixth gravity, so the men began to bounce their way around to the side of the lunar module, where the lunar rover was stored. They released the two bolts situated either side of one of the panels on the descent stage of the spacecraft. Fixed to the inside of this panel was a long nylon cord. This was threaded round a small pulley, which Martin began to play out from inside of the panel. Once the entire length of the cord was free Martin handed one end to Rossi.

"Got that, Dave?"

"Yes, I've got it. I'll take up the slack then you can release the final bolt," said the commander as he began to back away from the spacecraft. After taking several steps he pulled on the cord making it as tight as he could.

"Right, Stuart, release the bolt."

Martin lent forward and stretched out his right hand. Gripping the head of the bolt with his fingertips, he slowly released the final pin from the side panel. Rossi released the cord inch by inch, allowing the panel to fall gently to the ground, revealing the lunar rover which was stored inside.

"Okay, Stuart we're there."

"Right," said Martin. "I'll just release these restraining clips and the two slings then we'll lower it to the ground."

Leaning inside the spacecraft, he unclipped the rover from its restraining bar and began to uncoil the two slings.

"Okay, Dave, I'll be with you in a moment."

Martin looked across the lunar surface. Although the view was of a bleak barren world, the geologist was still fascinated at the sight before him. The mountains in the distance, the rocks scattered around him, and the undulations of the land made this desolate place a geologist's dream.

"Stuart, I hate to interrupt your sightseeing but we need to press on."

"Sorry, Dave. I just wanted a good look at what no one else has seen."

Martin bounced his way in the one sixth gravity across to Rossi who was playing out the two slings.

"Okay, Stu, you ready?"

"Sure, I'll take the left hand side, Dave," said Martin as he handed the right sling to his commander.

"Right, Stu, now don't forget to stand clear when she's at forty five degrees because the wheels spring into place rather suddenly."

"You don't have to remind me. The first time I did this in training those wheels almost took my head off."

"Okay, easy does it," said Rossi as both astronauts gently lowered the rover. The vehicles rear end continued to rotate downwards until suddenly the spring loaded wheels sprung into position.

"Didn't get you this time," laughed Rossi.

The rear wheels finally touched the surface of the moon.

"Outrigger cables are nice and loose," said Rossi. "Let's lower the left side a little."

Martin continued to release the left sling lowering the rover a couple of feet at a time until the front wheels sprang open.

"That's it, we're down now, Dave."

The vehicle was at last on the ground with the front pointing towards the spacecraft.

"Let's pull her away from the ship and then turn her a hundred and eighty degrees," said Rossi.

The lunar rover was a very lightweight machine. Lifting and turning it around was no problem in this gravity. Using the outboard handholds mounted either side of the chassis, the two men lifted the rover off the ground.

"Okay, Stuart, let's take it forward about ten feet then we'll turn it."

The two men carried the vehicle away from the lunar module, with their feet sinking into the grey powder-like landscape as they bounced their way along the surface.

"Right, Stu, that's far enough. Let's turn her around now."

As they began to turn one hundred and eighty degrees, both Rossi and Martin quickly realised that moving around on the moon was no easy feat.

"How are you doing, Dave? Are you finding things a little different from training?"

"You bet I am. Walking in a straight line isn't so bad, but turning in a circle isn't so easy. Still we're nearly there."

Once they'd turned the rover around, they gently lowered it to the ground. They were almost ready to start their journey to the dome. Both of them were anxious to finish the vehicle's construction so they could press on with the mission.

"Stuart, if you set up the film camera I'll tend to the seats."

"Roger that, Dave."

The seats and camera were held in their stowed position on the chassis with strips of Velcro. This was to prevent any movement during the flight and for easy storage in the descent stage of the lunar module. Martin crouched forward as far as his bulky spacesuit would allow. He stretched out his right hand and carefully peeled back a strip of Velcro used to hold a mono pod in a horizontal position. This was connected to a sixteen millimetre film camera to record the journey in the rover and to film the interior of the dome. The mono pod had a pivot at its base so the unit could be swung into a vertical position, then a spring loaded pin would slide into its stand locking the pod and camera into place.

"How are you doing, Stu?"

"Fine, the mono pod's moving into position nicely," said Martin as he slowly raised the camera into its vertical attitude. "I think the pin has locked itself into place. I'll just give it a little push."

The camera didn't move as Martin rocked the unit gently. It seemed the assembly was firmly in place and ready to be switched on when the astronauts were ready.

"Are the seats in position, Dave?"

"Yeah, I think we're ready to go." Rossi looked towards Martin for a moment. "All set?"

Martin turned and looked towards the dome. The great structure was beckoning.

"All set," he said eagerly.

They slowly climbed onto the lunar rover. Rossi, with his right hand on the inboard hand hold, pulled himself in and settled into his seat. Martin pushed himself upright, making sure he could reach the camera controls, then buckled his seat belt.

"Oh yeah," laughed Rossi. "Safety belts on. Watch out for traffic."

"Say, Dave, do you notice that in lunar gravity the suit doesn't compress nearly as much under our weight as it does on earth."

"Yes, I've noticed," said Rossi, but the commander wasn't interested in this, he just wanted to get the rover moving. Looking at the control console he began to switch on the power.

"Okay, circuit breakers in, amp-hours one hundred and five.

Volts eighty two, and battery temperature reading sixty eight."

"Right, Dave, copy that."

Rossi placed his hand around the controller and pushed it forward. Instantly four electric motors, one for each wheel, started to propel the rover across the landscape.

"Hey, does this little baby move!" said Martin, as the vehicle picked up speed to twelve kilometres an hour. The rover rocked from side to side as it travelled across the uneven ground. Its wheels sank into the grey lunar surface, churning up land which since the dawn of time had never seen sunlight.

"Switch the camera on, Stuart, we're getting close."

"Okay, Dave."

Both men looked up at the dome as they approached. The whole structure seemed to soar into the sky as they got closer, and the detail in the complex frame work became clearer. Its beautiful green glass shone in the sunlight and gave a welcoming feeling to the two men from Earth.

"Stuart, look. Many of the glass sections have been smashed," said Rossi.

"Yes, I wonder how long this thing's been here."

"Probably centuries. I'm going to look for a smashed section at ground level which we can drive the rover through. Keep your eyes peeled," said Rossi.

The lunar rover continued on towards the dome, with both men looking for a way in. As Martin looked across the base of the structure, a small shiny object caught his attention.

"Dave, look to the right. Over there, do you see it?" he said with great excitement.

Rossi looked and noticed the object sticking out of the moon's surface. He steered the rover towards it and as they approached they saw more pieces of metal scattered around a small area.

"Let's take a look," said Rossi.

The commander stopped the rover only feet from the debris. Neither of them moved or said anything for a moment, as they could see that this was not a part of the dome.

"It looks like wreckage of some sort," said Martin.

"You're right, but the wreckage of what?"

Rossi carefully climbed off the rover and made his way towards the largest piece. Martin followed as quickly as possible, taking care not to let his excitement get the better of him. Any movement that could cause him to fall would create a number of problems.

"God damn. Would you believe it," said Rossi. "I know what this is!"

"What?" shouted Martin? "What do you mean, you know what it is?"

Rossi carefully leaned forward and pulled a small piece of wreckage out of the ground. It was about fifteen inches square. He turned it around in his hands looking for any markings.

"Stuart, I know what this is!"

"What for God sake? Tell me!"

"You're looking at the remains of Surveyor 4."

"Surveyor 4?"

"Yes. In 1967 N.A.S.A sent surveyor probes to land on the moon. Their purpose was to land and take samples of the lunar surface."

"And?"

"Well some of them were successful, and others weren't. Surveyor 4 was the biggest mystery of all."

"Why, what happened?"

"Everything was going according to plan, but only minutes from landing all contact with the probe was lost."

"Retro failure?" said Martin.

"No, everything on the spacecraft was fine."

"Maybe it exploded."

"No, that didn't happen either, otherwise there would have been multiple blips on our radars. It just disappeared in an instant, and now you and I have discovered why." Martin nodded his head.

"It collided with the dome on its descent. Is that what you're saying?"

"Yes. I reckon the surveyor hit the dome as it was coming in to land. This would change the vehicles altitude, which meant the antenna relaying signals back to earth would have instantly been jarred out of position, resulting in an instant loss of reception. We 'll collect some pieces of this on the way back so it can be examined when we get home."

"Okay but let's get moving, Dave, I've got to get into that dome," said Martin eager to press on.

"Okay," said Rossi throwing the piece of the surveyor on the ground. "Well that solves the mystery of Surveyor 4. Now we better start solving the mystery of this thing," he said looking up at the great structure. "Come on, let's get moving."

They looked up at the magnificent edifice just yards away from them.

"This is some piece of work, isn't it, Dave?" said Martin as he gazed at the beautiful green tinted glass built into each of the hundreds of hexagon frames.

"It sure is, and I'm burning to find out what's inside. Come on, let's see if we can find an opening."

The astronauts made their way back to the lunar rover and climbed on board.

Rossi pushed the hand controller forward, immediately activating the rover's four electric drive wheel motors. The moon vehicle continued on its journey, as the astronauts guided it around the perimeter of the dome. After a few minutes, Martin noticed an opening.

"Dave look, about one hundred yards away," he said pointing to a smashed section which was at ground level.

"Yes I see it, and I think it's big enough to get the rover through."

Rossi steered the vehicle towards a large damaged section which they could use to enter the dome's interior. Bringing the rover to a standstill only yards away from the entrance, both astronauts leapt onto the moon's surface. They headed with great excitement towards the opening, their anticipation was high as they tried to imagine the contents of the dome. As they entered the structure, they suddenly stopped and stood motionless, saying nothing for a moment.

"I can't believe this," said Rossi slowly and with great disappointment. "I don't believe it."

There in front of them lay a one and a half mile diameter of lunar landscape, and nothing else. The dome was completely empty. The race to the moon between the United States of America and the Soviet Union had been for nothing, or at least it seemed that way. There was none of the advanced technology that Saltzman had hoped to capitalise on, just an empty shell. Martin looked up at the roof stretching high above him. Slowly his eyes moved across the area of the magnificent construction that surrounded him.

"Why would anybody want to build a place like this that serves no purpose, Dave?" he asked.

"Maybe there is a purpose to it. It's just that we haven't found it yet. Come on let's get back to the rover, I want to go further inside."

Rossi was convinced there was more to the dome than what they had seen. As they headed back to the rover, the commander felt an answer had to be somewhere inside the structure. Both astronauts fastened themselves into their seats, and Rossi soon had the vehicle moving towards the opening.

"How are we doing for battery power, Stu?"

Martin leaned forward and glanced at the instrument panel in front of him to check the battery gauge.

"We've plenty of power, Dave. If this thing is only a mile and a half in diameter, then we'll have power to reach the other side and back again, and still have plenty in reserve."

"Good," said Rossi. "I've got a feeling we're not going to have to travel that far."

They continued their journey into the interior of the dome. The ride on the rover was now much smoother as the lunar surface was flatter and free from boulders and rocks. It was obvious that the area had been levelled just as any construction worker would prepare the ground before laying any foundations. Martin looked up and around him as they were engulfed by the massive construction. He noticed that the green tinted glass absorbed the sunlight but had the capability of holding back the heat.

"Well, Dave, it's certainly not a greenhouse, that's for sure."

"You don't think so?" said Rossi.

"No, I was beginning to think that it could be some kind of biosphere for growing some plant life, but it's far too cold."

Suddenly Rossi noticed an object ahead of them that lay directly in the centre of the dome.

"Stuart look, about a hundred yards ahead."

"I see it," said Martin.

They steered the lunar rover directly towards the object. Bringing the vehicle to a stop only feet from it, both astronauts climbed off the rover and headed towards it. Then the two men stopped and stood motionless for what seemed an eternity as they looked in disbelief at what stood in front of them. Standing four feet high six feet long and three feet wide was a green marble block, but it was the object standing on top of it which transfixed the astronauts.

"Dave, do you see what I see?" asked Martin slowly.

"I can't believe this," said Rossi. "Who or what could have put that there?"

It was almost impossible for the two of them to comprehend what they were looking at, but this was for real. There, a quarter of a million miles from earth, standing eighteen inches high, was a solid gold crucifix. Rossi moved towards the marble block and picked up the cross. He rested it in the palm of his left hand and looked hard at its beautifully polished smooth surface. It had no engraving or markings on it as far as he could see. It was a simple cross about a quarter of an inch thick mounted on an eight inch square gold base. Did the cross mean the same to the alien race which built the dome as it did to Rossi, or was there another meaning to it?

"I wonder what Saltzman will make of this, Dave?" said Martin.

"I don't know, but it isn't what he was expecting, that's for sure."

Rossi looked around at the great dome, and marvelled at the magnificent structure.

He said quietly, "Stuart I think we may have discovered something more important than alien technology."

'That's for sure," said Martin as he moved closer to the marble block. Then he noticed that the top of this object was a separate block. He rested the palms of his hands on the edge of it and began to push. In the one sixth gravity it began to move easily. With great excitement he called out to Rossi, "Dave, this as a top, help me move it."

Rossi quickly began to help Martin push the top off what now appeared to be a marble casket.

Both men pushed until gradually this top piece fell over the back of the casket hitting the ground slowly and sending lunar dust gently it to the air.

They both looked inside the casket and were astonished at what they saw. Lying inside the casket were two stone tablets. The tablets were two feet in length, eighteen inches wide, and one inch thick. Martin reached inside and carefully lifted them out and began to wipe the dust from them. There was some kind of ancient writing on them which meant nothing to Rossi, but for an Archaeologist like Martin this was a revelation. He continued to wipe the tablets and he suddenly stopped. With his eyes wide open he glared at the stones. Rossi looked across at Martin and seeing the disbelief on the young man's face said.

"Stuart what is it, do you understand what it says?"

Martin eager to see more of the writings now wiped the stones with more vigour. He stopped and began to read to himself. Rossi looked at Martin again. He could see that the Archaeologist could understand the writing.

"Stuart will you please tell me what it says?"

Martin turned and looked straight at Rossi and in a calm voice said, "Dave, this is Hebrew."

There was a moment's pause as the two men looked at each other, then Martin made an unbelievable statement. "Dave, these are the TEN COMMANDMENTS."

Rossi stood speechless as he looked at the tablets. "Are you sure?" he said in disbelief.

"Yes, yes I'm sure, Dave, I know I'm right."

Rossi, still shocked at what Martin had just revealed to him, said, "Stuart have you any Idea what this could mean?"

"Dave, at this point in time I haven't got a clue what any of this means, but what I do know is that some of our history is going to have to be rewritten."

Rossi leant forward and looked into the marble casket again. Carefully placed at the corner was what looked like a large leather sack. Carefully leaning into the casket as not to damage or tear his spacesuit, Rossi carefully reached for the bag, and grabbing it with his fingertips he slowly lifted it out of the casket.

"What have we got here?" he said as he opened the large bag. He reached inside and pull out a book. It was ten inches high eight inches wide and two inches thick. Wiping what little dust had formed on the cover, Rossi open it and looked at the writing on the page. With his eyes wide open he stood in total disbelief.

"This is written in Russian." He said looking at Martin. He began to open the book glancing quickly at each page. 'Yes the whole thing is written in Russian."

"God damn," said Martin. "Have we been had?"

Rossi quickly lay the book on the edge of the casket and pulled another book from the bag. It was identical to the first. He opened it and looked at the pages.

"Stu, look at this, it's written in Spanish." He handed it to Martin. "Here take a look for yourself."

Martin couldn't believe it, but sure enough his commander was right. The entire book was written in Spanish. Rossi, his mind racing trying to work out what the whole structure was about, said, "What the hell gives?"

"I don't know," replied Martin, "but I don't think that we will find the answer here. We have to get these books back to Earth to be examined further."

"Okay, let's get out of here and back to the ship," said Rossi. "I'm sure there's nothing else here for us."

"Right, Dave. I wouldn't mind collecting some pieces of the broken glass and taking it back to earth for analysis if we've got time."

"Okay, that's fine by me. Let's get going."

Both men returned to the rover and climbed on board. Martin rested the bag containing the books and cross on his knees, while Rossi switched on the power to the rover.

"Just check the battery power for me, Stu."

Martin glanced at the control panel and towards the battery volt meter.

"Yes, we're okay, Dave, we've got more than enough power to stop and pick up some glass before carrying on to the lunar module."

Rossi put the rover into forward drive. As the tiny vehicle began to move, he drove as fast as he could go. He followed the tracks that the rover had made on its inbound journey back to the point where they had entered the dome.

"Stuart, I'm going to stop by the wreckage of Surveyor 4. There are pieces of broken glass around that area. If you collect the glass I'll gather some fragments of the Surveyor. There's a certain piece I want to look for and take back to earth."

"Okay, Dave, no problem."

Rossi steered the rover out of the dome. As he followed the wheel tracks around its perimeter, it wasn't long before the wreckage of Surveyor 4 came into sight.

"Stuart, you collect as much broken glass as you can, while I look for that piece of Surveyor I want."

"Right, Dave," said Martin, as they brought the lunar rover to a halt.

Rossi took a pair of specially made mechanical grips which were used to pick up rock samples from the lunar surface, and headed for the crash site of the Surveyor. There were many pieces of the dome's broken glass lying amongst the destroyed spacecraft, so neither of the astronauts had to stray away from each other as they set about collecting the artefacts.

The first piece of wreckage Rossi picked up was the antenna which the Surveyor used to send back its signals to earth. He then began to look for what he considered to be the most important part of the spacecraft.

"Dave, I think we have enough pieces of glass to take with us," said Martin as he moved towards his commanding officer.

"Right, Stu. There's just this one piece of the surveyor I have to find."

As Rossi looked around the area he noticed a cylinder protruding out of the lunar surface.

"Yes, I think that could be it."

He moved towards the part of the spacecraft he was eager to examine and began to pull it from under the moon's surface with the mechanical grips. About four inches of the component had been buried, but now Rossi had retrieved this vital part of the surveyor.

"What's that?" asked Martin.

"This is the Vernier rocket cluster," said Rossi as he looked carefully at the small retro engines. "These should have ignited as the Surveyor made its final approach."

"Did they?"

"They didn't have time. The craft hit the dome before they had a chance to fire. This is why the craft instantly lost contact with earth because its antenna was moved into another position."

"I suppose that clears that incident up, Dave," said Martin.

"Sure does. I wanted to find this component to prove to everyone back home that it wasn't the spacecraft that failed. The mystery of Surveyor 4 and its sudden disappearance lay in the existence of this Dome."

Rossi paused for a moment and looked up at the great dome with great admiration for the race of people that built it.

"Incredible," he said quietly, then wakening from his day dreaming turned to Martin and said, "Okay, now have you got enough glass?"

"Yeah, I think this should be enough for our scientists to examine."

"Right, let's get back to the lunar module."

The men wasted no time climbing back on the vehicle. Once again Rossi followed the tracks of the moon vehicle back to Europa. As they approached the spacecraft he checked his watch.

"Stuart that pre-recorded tape should have stopped transmitting that phony mission of ours."

"Yes, I just hope that the world's media will buy that story about our video antenna breaking down."

Rossi stopped the rover only feet away from the ladder of the lunar module.

"Right, I'll open the hatch while you detach the film camera."

"Okay, Dave, will do," replied Martin.

Rossi bounced his way to the foot of the ladder in the one sixth gravity. With his left arm wrapped firmly around the small cylindrical Vernier engine he climbed towards the ascent stage of the spacecraft.

Martin released the pin holding the film camera on the mono pod and then carefully lifted it from its stand.

"Dave, I'm going to make a couple of journeys. When you've opened the hatch you climb in and I'll pass everything to you. I'll hand you the camera first then I'll come back for everything else."

"Roger that, Stu. Don't forget anything."

"Okay I'll make three journeys."

Rossi was now at the top of the ladder. He reached for the lever on the hatch. Pulling it downwards he pushed the small door open.

"Everything okay, Dave?" asked Martin.

"Yes, hatch open. I'm just going to put the Vernier engine inside then you can climb up and pass me everything else."

Rossi pushed the small rocket motor into the lunar module then eased himself into spacecraft.

"Right, do you want to start making your way up?"

"Sure," replied Martin.

Carefully holding the camera and surveyor's antenna under his right arm, Martin began to climb the ladder.

"How we doing for time, Dave?"

"I'm afraid our recording has run out. Once you're in the ship we'll make contact with control, then I'll find out where Andrew is."

"Don't forget, Dave, I've got to make another journey for the other three items," said Martin as he continued to climb the ladder of the lunar module.

"Okay, no problem, carry on," replied Rossi.

Back at the control centre at Cape Kennedy, Vigo Saltzman was coming to the end of a gruelling press conference. He stood behind a small lectern mounted on a three foot high platform which overlooked members of the media. He'd been questioned for some time, but the cunning industrialist had not let much slip about his mission. A young blond-haired girl in her early twenties raised her hand to ask a question.

"Mr Saltzman, my name's Janet Hartson of Life magazine. There's been no radio contact for thirty minutes with Commander Rossi and Stuart Martin, yet you don't seem to be too concerned about this. Can I ask you why that is?"

"Well Miss Hartson, there was a ninety minute transmission from Commander Rossi before contact was lost. He told us the high gain antenna on the lunar module was causing problems, so we believe this is the reason for loss of signal. We don't believe our astronauts are in any danger."

Then a journalist with more experience than Miss Hartson raised his hand. This was a man who wasn't so easily thrown by deceit as his young colleague.

"Mr Saltzman, Geoff Hannon from the New York Times. I've been told that you're some kind of Howard Hughes, a man the public sees very little of. Is that right, sir?"

"Well, first of all, Mr Hannon, can I thank you for likening me to Howard Hughes," laughed Saltzman. "As for the public, well, I spend most of my time working. I'm a very busy man, Mr Hannon, I have many subsidiary companies I have to attend to and that takes up a lot of my time."

Hannon gave a polite smile before asking his next question. "You tell us this mission is to find a rare mineral?"

"That's right," replied Saltzman.

"Can you tell us how you knew it was there?"

"Yes. Before the Apollo missions began, the surveyor spacecraft's landed on the moon to test the lunar surface."

Before Saltzman could finish what he was saying Hannon came in with another question.

"And was a surveyor spacecraft sent to the Sinus Medii, Mr Saltzman?"

"Yes, that's how we discovered the mineral, Mr Hannon."

"Really?" pressed Hannon. "I was lead to believe Surveyor 4 stopped transmitting as it was descending to the lunar surface. So I ask again, how did you discover this so called mineral?"

There was total silence in the room as Saltzman's smug smile was wiped from his face.

"Well, I do believe Mr Hannon, there were other missions," said Saltzman in a very unsure way.

"Mr Saltzman, forgive me, sir, but I don't believe this story about some mineral on the moon," said Hannon. "Your company builds aircraft for the military. I doubt whether you're the sort of man who would spend your millions on an Apollo mission looking for moon rock."

There was total silence in the room as members of the press and TV waited for Saltzman's answer. He stood speechless and embarrassed for a moment, and then as if his prayers were answered, the crackling sound of the radio echoed around the control centre.

"Europa to Cap-com do you read? Over."

The sound of Dave Rossi's voice brought Saltzman the escape he needed from the pressures of the media.

"Roger Europa," declared a relieved capsule communicator, Frank Gregg. "Where have you been, Dave?"

On board the lunar module Europa, Rossi and Martin had closed the hatch of their spacecraft and were preparing for their ascent from the lunar surface.

"We're sorry for the delay Houston, but we think we've managed to repair the high gain antenna," said Rossi.

The control room personnel knew that all this was staged, but it was all part of the plan.

"Well it's great to hear your voice again, Dave," said Gregg.

"Did you find anything while you were on the surface?"

"We sure did. We've found a blue coloured rock. It looks a little like sapphire and warrants extensive testing."

Immediately Saltzman turned towards the members of the press.

"You see, Mr Hannon, I told you there was a rare mineral on the moon. Now perhaps you and the rest of your so-called professionals would keep out of my way in future," said Saltzman viciously. "We have three astronauts to bring home, so if you don't mind I will ask you all to leave the premises. Show them out someone."

Saltzman turned away from the group and began to walk briskly towards the control desk manned by Gregg. A security guard approached the journalists and in a quiet voice said, "Ladies and gentlemen if you'd like to follow me please, I'll escort you from the building."

Quietly they turned and followed the security guard towards the exit door, all except for Hannon. He stood for a few moments staring across the control centre. He had a hunch that the story he and his colleagues had been told just wasn't right. He couldn't prove otherwise of course. He turned around and made his way to the exit, determined that one day he'd find out the truth, but it wouldn't be today.

"Now gentlemen, let's get in touch with Andrew Wilson in the command module," said Saltzman. "The sooner we get them home the quicker we'll find out what they've discovered."

Gregg swivelled his chair around and pulled himself towards his desk.

"Cap-com to Titan, cap-com to Titan do you receive? Over."

Orbiting sixty nautical miles above the lunar surface, the command module Titan had emerged from the far side of the moon. In the weightless environment of space Andrew Wilson floated across the control cabin towards the radio. It was a welcoming call as he'd been totally alone for the last two hours, forbidden to make contact with earth and his fellow astronauts.

"Roger cap-com, this is Titan reading you loud and clear Frank," came the calm voice of Wilson.

"Dave and Stuart are ready to begin their ascent Andrew."

"Roger, will be in range in approximately twenty minutes."

"Copy that Titan. Cap-com to Europa, Andrew will be in range in twenty minutes, Dave."

Inside the lunar module Rossi and Martin were making the final checks for their ascent.

"Copy that cap-com, we'll be ready," said Rossi. "Okay, how are we doing, Stu?

"Fine, Dave, circuit breakers in, T.C.A throttle to maximum, ascent engine armed."

"Roger, starting final countdown. T minus twenty and counting."

As the minutes passed away, Saltzman, Professor Steiner and the mission control technicians waited anxiously for Europa's ascent engine to fire.

With his hands gripping the control lever Rossi continue the countdown. "Five, four, three, two, one, ignition."

Immediately the lunar module's ascent engine exploded into life. Debris from the descent stage flew in all directions as the two sections of the spacecraft separated.

"We have lift-off Huston," called out Rossi. "Rate of climb two hundred feet per second."

As Europa began to climb into the blackness of space, Martin took a few moments to peer out of his window. The dome gradually became smaller in the distance as the lunar module raced into orbit, yaw and pitching into position for its rendezvous with the command module. The geologist had spent many months training for this mission to spend just a few hours on the moon. The hard work had been worth it, he thought to himself. Along with Rossi he had seen something that no other human being had ever witnessed. The fragments of the green coloured glass which made up the dome's outer shell would be examined by him and Saltzman's team. Then there were the tablets of stone with the Ten Commandments. The books, ten of them in total, all of this was a far greater discovery than advanced weapons thought Martin. He looked forward to finding out what all of this had meant to the aliens who had built the dome. It was obvious that these people shared something in common with the human race back on earth, but what would it be.

chapter seven

THE SECRET OF LIFE

It had been two months since the crew of Apollo 18 returned to Earth, a time in which Saltzman and his team of scientists had examined the books and green tinted glass which had made up the outer shell of the alien dome which had been discovered on the moon.

In the underground room at area 51, Curtis, Rossi, Colonel John Gorman and James Hoffman, sat waiting patiently for Vigo Saltzman and Professor Steiner to report their findings to the group.

"Do you think they've had enough time to examine the artefacts thoroughly chief, after all two months to study those books doesn't seem a long time to me?" said Curtis.

Hoffman, knowing Saltzman like he did, replied, "Oh I bet Vigo has had his staff working round the clock to uncover what those books mean."

"I don't think he would have called us here today Steve if he didn't have something important to tell us," said Rossi.

Suddenly the sound of the elevator descending broke the silence in the room. The four men rose from their seats and waited with great anticipation for Saltzman and Steiner. The elevator stopped with a gentle thud and instantly the doors slid open. Saltzman with his usual powerful ego wasted no time as he stormed into the room leaving Steiner in his wake.

"Gentlemen, it's good to see you all again," he said with great excitement. "Please sit down all of you. I have some amazing revelations for you."

The four men sat down as Steiner joined Salzman at the front of the room. He placed the English translation of one of the books on the table in front of him, composed himself, then took a deep breath.

"Gentlemen, it has taken us almost ten years to retrieve the contents of the alien dome on the moon." Saltzman then started to walk back and forth in front of the group in his familiar way.

"We had expected to find advanced technology which we hoped could be useful for our countries defence…"

"You mean YOU hoped to find advanced technology," interrupted Curtis as he reminded the industrialist that the whole expedition was organized by him for that sole purpose. Saltzman, not liking Curtis's remark, but accepted it, because he was eager to move on.

"Yes, yes Steve all right it's what I had hoped for, but nevertheless what the Apollo crew found was ten identical books all in different languages, the one written in English here in front of me. It's as if the aliens wanted every person on this earth to read about their experiences."

"What experience's Vigo?" said Gorman.

"Experiences that were completely parallel to ours, Colonel, well up to a certain point in time."

"Parallel to ours?" said Rossi. "What do you mean?"

"These books tell us about a race of people known as the Jardan who lived, or may still live as far as we know, on the planet K7.43 which orbits a star approximately five light years from Earth. I say parallel, Mr Rossi, because every person they talk about in this book has lived on this Earth."

"What?" said Hoffman in disbelief. "Lived on this earth?"

"Yes, Mr Hoffman, where people on this world have a double, on an identical world."

"Okay, yes, I've heard of that notion but that's all it is," said Hoffman, a man who still liked facts and not conjecture and other people's theories.

"A parallel world James." said Steiner. The German was eager to explain the beliefs he and his fellow scientists had discussed back in Germany in the nineteen twenties.

"Before the war started I met a fellow student at university named Bernhardt Meyer. He was brilliant. He had a theory that the universe was so big that the law of average's would mean that there could be thousands of earth type planets."

"Oh yes, earth like planets, I can accept that," said Curtis, "but that's not identical, is it?"

Steiner continued, "No, Steve, but Meyer, like many scientists believed that space time is flat. If that's so, then space time goes on forever, and if that's accurate it means at some point space time must repeat itself."

Rossi was now beginning to understand a little of what the Professor was saying. He said, "So if space time repeats it self, eventually I would encounter another version of me."

"Correct, Dave," said Steiner.

Gorman sat up in his chair and said, "So everything that happens here on earth can happen in the same way somewhere else."

"Yes it can," said Steiner, "but in this case there was a dramatic change of fortune."

"What do you mean professor a change of fortune?" said Hoffman.

"James, imagine the planet earth at the time of the dinosaurs and another world, a parallel world with dinosaurs that were doppelgangers of ours."

"Okay," said Hoffman slowly, as he tried desperately to follow the professor.

"Now imagine our planet being hit by an asteroid and wiping out our dinosaurs, BUT it didn't happen to the parallel world. This means a change in direction for both planets.

There was a moments silence from the group before Hoffman answered. "Yes I see what you mean."

"And from the information you've obtained from these books your saying that this has happened here, is that correct?" asked Curtis.

"Correct," said Saltzman as he took over the conversation. "That's exactly what happened."

Gorman, accepting this idea, wanted to know more, "And this direction change with our planet and the aliens, when did that take place?"

Saltzman looked at Steiner for a brief moment. He knew what he was about to say would astonish the group, nevertheless he took a breath and with a loud voice said.

"It was at the crucifixion of Christ colonel, that's where the parallel ended and the two planets took a different course to each other."

There was total silence in the room as the group tried to get their minds focused on what they'd been told. Curtis, being a Christian man was eager to know were Christ fitted into all of this. He sat up on the couch were he sat next to Hoffman.

"Do the books actually tell you all of this Salzman?" he asked.

"Read it for yourself if you wish, Mr Curtis and you'll see that our worlds were identical up to that point in time. There was an Adam and Eve, Abraham, the great exodus from Egypt lead by Moses and the rise of Israel."

Curtis was still confused at all of this. He stood up and walked to the table were Saltzman had placed the book. He picked it up and began to read a section of the first page to himself.

"Are we saying that Jesus has a doppelganger too?"

Steiner smiled, "No Steve, Jesus is the Christ, there's only one of him.

"So how was Jesus on planet K7.43 and ours at the same time?"

"Good question." replied Steiner. The German scientist rubbed the palm of his right hand against his chin, thinking hard about how he was to explain the next point.

"Well Steve, this is where it starts to get a little heavy. You see according from what we can work out from these books, planet K7.43, although parallel to our earth is one thousand years ahead of us."

"Oh my God, now that is what I call heavy." said Rossi placing his hand on his forehead and slumping back in the couch in complete confusion. Hoffman just as mystified, tried desperately to understand, "So you're telling us that in our universe there could be hundreds of planets that are parallel to each other but all living on a different time line?"

"Correct James. I'm afraid to say even the greatest minds have yet to work all of this out."

"All right let's leave the science to the scientists," said Gorman. "You said that K7.43 and Earth changed from the moment Christ was crucified, WHY?"

Saltzman walked directly in front of the group and said, "Because the Jardan accepted Christ and all his teaching while we rejected and murdered him, that's why, Mr Gorman. From that moment this race of people gained knowledge beyond their wildest dreams."

"In what way?" asked Gorman.

"Because all conflict became a thing of the past and the Jardan put their time and effort into more profitable projects rather than finding ways to destroy each other like we do."

"And the dome on the moon, where does that come into the story?" asked Rossi.

"According to these books the Jardan became one of the most advanced races in the universe. Their scientist developed techniques into bending space making traveling through the cosmos routine. Then they discovered

Earth and built the dome on the moon as an observation station. This was at a time when the human race were building the pyramids in Egypt. They made constant visits to Earth and observed the birth of Christ but were forbidden to intervene in any of the events in his life, even in his death."

Steiner then took over from Saltzman. "It was when the human race detonated the first atom bomb, the Jardan really became concerned about our future. They made more visits to Earth and tried to make some attempt to change our course, but only to find we'd reached a stage in our development where we could be a danger to even them. So they decided to leave us and allow us to make the final decision on our future and existence. Knowing that one day we would reach the level of primitive space travel, they left the moon leaving the books and dome behide so we could discover them."

"And the Ten Commandments, what about them?" asked Rossi.

"They were left in order for us to try and understand that the laws of God apply not just to us, but to every world and race in the universe.

Curtis, standing next to Saltzman with the book gripped in his hand, said, "We can stand here and talk all day long about this, but it's obvious to me what this is all about. It's about a race of people who became magnificent and achieved marvels because they put Christ at the forefront of their decision making, and they have tried to make it known to us that by knowing God we can achieve the same thing."

Curtis took his eyes away from the pages of the book, looked up to address the group and said.

"Gentlemen, with a world that is parallel to ours, it proves that it's not beyond us to become like the Jardan. If man can make a case for war, then he his capable of making a case for peace. It won't be by guns and missiles that will bring salvation to our world, but it will be by the laws of God, for while man persists in waging war he deprives himself of progress. What do YOU think?"